The
Golden Warrior
and the
Plot to Kill
George Washington

By Stephen Sparacio, Sr.

Order this book online at www.trafford.com
or email orders@trafford.com

Most Trafford titles are also available at major online book retailers.

Printed in Victoria, BC, Canada.

ISBN: 978-1-4269-0464-6 (sc)
ISBN: 978-1-4269-0465-3 (hc)
ISBN: 978-1-4269-3207-6 (eb)

Library of Congress Control Number: 2010908340

*Our mission is to efficiently provide the world's finest, most comprehensive book publishing
service, enabling every author to experience success. To find out how to publish your book, your
way, and have it available worldwide, visit us online at www.trafford.com*

Trafford rev. 06/08/2010

www.trafford.com

North America & international
toll-free: 1 888 232 4444 (USA & Canada)
phone: 250 383 6864 ✦ fax: 812 355 4082

DEDICATION

To my wife Lucille for her love, inspiration, and encouragement without which this novel would not exist.

For my daughter, Suzanne Soetje, for her expert typing of most of the original manuscript and her always cheerful words of encouragement.

For my son, Stephen Paul Jr., for his excellent efforts to do whatever he could to help me.

For my son-in-law, Frederick Soetje, for his help in ascertaining some research, in checking corrections, and in typing part of the original manuscript.

And for that friend and neighbor, now long gone, who first told me the story of the unusual and beautiful Indian Princess – Arandel.

◆◆◆

Contents

PREFACE

"When we forget contributors to our American History – when we neglect the heroic past of the American Indian – We thereby weaken our own heritage. We need to remember the contributions our forefathers found here and from which they borrowed liberally."

John F. Kennedy
President of the United States

♦♦♦

Much of the following story is based on either historical fact or legendary tales. But, since it is still a work of fiction, it also doesn't claim to be historically accurate in every detail.

It does, however, attempt to capture the spirit of the Long Island Indians and patriots during the American Revolution – and to dispel some of the misjudgments about the Long Island Indians who, basically, were hard working and peaceful people.

It is also about the unsung heroism of the man who thwarted the British – Indian renegade plot to kill George Washington.

But, above all, it is a love story.

♦♦♦

As James Whitcomb Riley wrote:

Oh! Tell me a tale of the early days,
Of the times as they used to be."

S.S.

Introduction

When I was twelve years old, a friend and neighbor told me the story of the Indian Princess Arandel of the Massapequas tribe who, in the mid-1700's, lived in wigwams a few miles from my then home in Roosevelt, Long Island.

Many years later, out of curiosity, I researched the Algonquin Arandel and her lover, Nathaniel Townsend, and I found only several brief references to her. The research also hinted at a secret government file on Townsend.

Since then, whether their story was true, legend, myth, or completely fictional, I still wonder what would have happened if Nathaniel had turned around and...

S.S.

♦♦♦

PROLOGUE

Every time Nathaniel would later walk along those same woodland trails, he would be reminded of how she used to smile and laugh at his attempts to speak the Algonquin language and his romantic earnestness in gathering wild flowers for her. She would hold the multi-colored flowers, however, as if there were no greater treasure.

He couldn't forget Arandel's face and her smile, and all of those loving memories he remembered in his ten years with her. Many times in the night he would wake up sweating and sobbing, "Why didn't I turn around, if only I had..." - and the pain again would become unbearable...

◆◆◆

CHAPTER I

RENEGADE INDIANS

Even from a mile away, Nathaniel Townsend, recently recruited Army Scout and undercover colonial spy, could hear the fire of the long muzzle-loading flintlock muskets of the villagers.

Unfortunately, he could also hear the war cries of marauding Indians and the bone-chilling screams of their victims in the small settlement situated in the middle of the island and fifteen miles north of the Atlantic Ocean. The Indians apparently had to be renegades since the Algonquins on Long Island (Paumanok) in 1771 were known to be gentle, peaceful, and friendly in their relationships with the many English and the few Dutch settlers.

In his military briefings, Nathaniel was told that the high-ranking British officers were trying to get the support of the thirteen Algonquin subtribes by provoking the settlers to retaliate against the random attacks of the few non-tribal Indian renegades living on Long Island or recruited from the isolated areas along the Connecticut River across the "Bay," which was the Indian name for the Long Island Sound. It was believed that such renegade attacks were intended to alienate the settlers against the tribal Algonquins who might then in retaliation decide to side with the British in case of war. The British, according to the rumor, were bribing the Indian mercenaries with wampum, liquor, tobacco, cheap but colorful trinkets, and sometimes with whalebone, which could be used for making weapons, such as clubs, knives, and various tools.

Three months ago, Nathaniel had his first experience, near Commack ("good land"), with the renegades who destroyed colonial homes, plundered, and killed all of the village inhabitants except a few settlers and one baby. One infant, placed under a bed by its protective mother, was able to survive. Nathaniel had come then upon the horrible and unforgettable scene: lying in grotesque positions were men, women, and children, who had been scalped after being killed either by arrows let loose from a long distance or by knives or tomahawks wielded in close combat. The arrows, tipped with shaped quartz or the sharpened antlers of deer, could easily penetrate deep into the victim's body.

Nathaniel later tried to dismiss these initial nightmarish visions and replace them with more pleasant memories of Arandel – the beautiful Arandel – and of his "second father," Chief Tackapousha of the Massapequas. Many evenings during his ten-year stay at the Chief's camp, he would banter with Arandel, sometimes boldly putting his arm around her waist, and listening enthralled as the Chief at evening campfires told stories about the "glorious" history of the Algonquins in the 1500's and 1600's.

Perpetuating the Indian tradition of communicating oral history, the Chief would recall the names of the many sachems then and how the early island Indians had cultivated the fertile land and survived through planting, hunting, and fishing. The waterways then were so abundant with fish, and to some extent still so now, that an Indian could easily scoop with his hands many fish from the streams and rivers and then put them into weaved baskets.

The Chief estimated that from the more than 6,000 Algonquins living on Paumanok in the 1500's and 1600's there were probably now fewer than one-third left because of illness such as smallpox, Indian wars, and fewer Indian marriages. But, each Indian village in the mid-1700's still contained at least 30 to 40 wigwams and one or two large wood lodges.

Turning his thoughts to the current British situation, Nathaniel knew that the British troops in 1771 were planning a campaign to invade and control Long Island in order to seize many of its resources, including cattle, crops, horses, and whale oil and whalebone. The British, through excessive taxation and military intimidation and force, were trying to subdue and dominate the colonial patriots who objected to the strict rules imposed by the British government 3,000 miles away.

King George III in 1765 had sent British soldiers to help the colonists fight the French settlers and those colonists who allied themselves with the French. The cost exceeded 60 million pounds which King George III tried to recoup by levying numerous taxes on those whom he described as "British citizens" in the New World.

Three years later, in 1768, four more British regiments had sailed from England to intimidate and quiet the rebellious English settlers. In 1770, after the British had forcefully occupied Boston, they endured a barrage of verbal criticism and physical assaults by the colonials. As a result, British governors were eventually sent to oversee and control settlers in each of the thirteen colonies.

Nathaniel recently had been told by his quasi - military superiors that formation of an established Continental Army was planned and that George Washington, a hero of the French and Indian War, was officially going to be named Commander-in-Chief.

The Continental Army to be established in 1774, or possibly even earlier, was expected to be one of the first creations of the 1st Continental Congress which would be formed to protect settlers. The Continental Congress would have the authority to eliminate all trade with England if the liberty and rights for colonists were not achieved. All of these thoughts about unwanted British intervention occupied Nathaniel's mind as he walked briskly and nervously to the site of the second renegade Indian attack.

Nathaniel, after recalling what had happened in the first renegade Indian attack three months ago, knew that he would soon see a similar sight in the nearby village, as he rounded a bend in the forest path. As he stepped over a large fallen branch of a birch tree, a grey, bushy-tailed racoon darted in front of him before scampering into the shrub. The raccoon's flight reminded him of the first attack and the survivors' accounts of the Indian renegades seemingly vanishing on horseback into the woods or racing across the plains after striking, killing, and plundering.

Breathing very hard, Nathaniel still did not regret walking instead of riding his horse. Trying again to recapture the past, even at this fearful moment, he would imagine that Arandel was there beside him, peacefully telling him the names of flowers and trees as well as the feeding and hiding habits of the wild animals. Life was so wonderful then - so beautiful, so kind.

Then, his mind couldn't reconcile the present with the past, and in a flashback, he again remembered the first incident three months ago that caused him so many sleepless nights – and which may again be repeated a hundred yards ahead of him.

Chapter 2

Nightmare

Just before he reached the second attacked village, he remembered the sight three months ago of the tall Indian warrior holding the scalp of a dying man – a scene which was even more grotesque and irrational because it contradicted his knowledge of the peaceful and non – violent Indians he knew as a youth growing up in Chief Tackapousha's village.

His Indian friends in the Chief's settlement, like most Algonquins, had long, straight black hair and brownish skin, and they had delighted in teasing Nathaniel, their blond – haired, "pale face" friend. The Massapequans were tall, about six feet, muscular because of all the running they did, and had stern and stoic facial expressions, which belied their kind and compassionate nature.

New settlers were sometimes unduly frightened by the Algonquins' dark eyes, which seemed menacing, and their black hair which was usually coated with foul-smelling bear grease. Their faces and bodies were marked with multi-colored dyes, principally red and yellow, which happened to be the traditional colors of the Massapequan clan. Nathaniel could not forget how Arandel would usually unsuccessfully try to put red and yellow dyed feathers in his blond hair. Sometimes she would take out the red and yellow feathers from her own hair and tickle him with them if he objected to wearing the feathers she had made especially for him.

In times of war, island Indian warriors would shave their heads, except for a two-inch wide and long narrow strip of hair from above their forehead to the nape of the neck. The "scalp lock" was a challenge to the enemy to try to remove it if one dared or thought he had the ability to do so.

Three months ago, Nathaniel's experience with the renegade warrior wearing a "scalp lock" was so unlike his more realistic understanding of and relationship with the placid Long Island Indians. The warrior then had dropped the scalp, again removed the tomahawk attached to his breech belt, and moved toward Nathaniel. Without hesitation, Nathaniel had unsheathed his long knife and with the expertise borne out of confidence of the hours and hours of past training he had, he hurled it at the warrior who clutched his chest and fell backward. With some difficulty, he extracted the knife, which was special since it was one of Chief Tackapousha's parting gifts. Nathaniel had trembled as he looked down at the dead enemy warrior lying next to the scalp of a white man who also had just died.

CHAPTER 3
KINDLY ACT

Knowing there was nothing he could do upon arriving at the site of the second renegade Indian attack, he surveyed the situation and then sadly walked back to report this similar Indian incident to his military contact. First, he would stop at his cottage, rest, and then mount his horse and travel the few miles to Fort Neck which was two miles west of Commack where he would confer with his immediate superior, Benjamin Tallmadge, a chief spy for what would eventually be the Continental Army.

As he moved along the winding trail, he reminisced about how Whaleman and Shanghai Jim, his two best friends, used to marvel at his extensive knowledge of the multi-colored woodland flowers and the more than dozen different varieties of trees. With ease, Nathaniel could identify the many island flowers: the white and pink daisies, purplish hyacinth, ground cherry laurel, white and purple lilies, pansies, red roses, tulips, reddish-blue violets, and so many more. Arandel, who had taught him the names of the wild flowers and trees, described them in a way he would never forget: "Nathaniel, don't you love the smell of flowers and the tall trees, as you pass by them? I call them creators of nature's woodland perfume."

them at their jointly-owned tavern after he made his military report. He would ride to the tavern located about four miles northeast of Nathaniel's cabin, which was several miles north of Chief Tackapousha's village.

As he rounded a turn in the trail, he saw that it was cluttered with fallen pine cones. He knew that the pine cone and pine tree were highly respected and valued by the Algonquins. Favorites of Indian children were the tree's outer layer, which contained a flavorful resin, and the green pine cones, which were roasted and then eaten. Nathaniel smiled as he remembered that the white settlers called the Algonquins "tree eaters." Nathaniel walked around the fallen pine cones, in respect for the mystical and practical significance it had for Chief Tackapousha's Algonquins, whom he liked to call his "second family."

After walking only a few yards, he looked ahead of him and saw a young Indian, probably sixteen or seventeen years old, slumped against the trunk of an oak tree. Not knowing what to expect, the boy looked menacingly at Nathaniel. As Nathaniel reached for his long knife, he approached the trembling boy. Like most stoic Indians, he tried to conceal his fear and pain. He used his left hand to cover a wound that could have been caused by musket fire, knife, or tomahawk. Nathaniel could see the blood falling steadily down his right arm. The young Brave, wanting to avoid capture or death, fumbled trying to reach the tomahawk under his belt and on his hip. But, the loss of blood and the exertion proved too much for him, and he fainted.

Upon awakening a few moments later, the young Brave frantically, but vainly, searched for his tomahawk, which Nathaniel had already discarded. Shaking but still defiant, the young Brave became calmer when he saw that Nathaniel was cleaning and then bandaging his

8

wound with a long, narrow bandana. Nathaniel had correctly identified the boy as a member of the far eastern Montauk tribe, because of the characteristic three yellow feathers in his hair and the bright black and yellow designs on his face and body.

The Montauks, one of the most powerful tribes on the island in the late 1600's and early 1700's, were now regarded as an extremely peaceful tribe ever since the death of their great sachem, Wyandanch. The only Indians more powerful than the Montauks in the 1600's were the cruel Pequots from eastern Connecticut who, like the Iroquois, expected yearly tribute from the Montauks and other subtribes. The wounded young warrior, near adulthood, was an anomaly – perhaps, thought Nathaniel, a Montauk who was exiled, for some reason, from his clan.

Located in and to the north of Manhattan, the Iroquois also were known once or twice a year to force tribute from the Canarsies subtribe situated just across the East River. More than a decade ago, one such Iroquois demand for a tribute had greatly changed the course of Nathaniel's life.

Nathaniel, momentarily distracted from bandaging the wound, saw that the facial expression of the young boy had become less hostile and more tranquil. After Nathanial finished, the young Montauk, realizing that he was not going to be detained or harmed, backed away slowly. As he looked at Nathaniel intensely, he vowed not to forget the help of this unusually kind white man before he quickly disappeared into the dark, thick foliage.

CHAPTER 4
FAME

The conflict between the British and the colonials had been steadily increasing since 1765 when Patrick Henry in the Virginia House of Burgesses declared that Virginians should be taxed by the Virginians and not by the British.

Seven years later, 1772, in The Old Tavern, which periodically was the meeting place of the patriotic colonial Sons of Liberty, the three owners almost every evening would discuss the latest news. Ironically, during the French and Indian war, also called Queen Anne's war, 1754-1763, the British and colonials sided with each other against the royal French troops and various Indian groups.

The full-scale battles and lesser skirmishes in the early 1770's mainly took place from Lake Ontario near Canada to the northern border of the colony of Virginia. Long Island, for the most part, was spared major military involvement.

British troops had originally been concentrated in three places - on Manhattan Island, near or in the town of Boston, and in the upper Hudson Valley. On Long Island, the British were mainly clustered for most of the duration of the Revolutionary War along the north shore in the far eastern end of the island where they had seized many whaling vessels and any whaling products they could expropriate for the war

effort, particularly favoring whalebone, whale oil, and whale sperm.
The captured colonial vessels were subsequently taken to Manhattan
Island where they were used either as prison ships for captured Patriots
or hospitals for sick or injured British soldiers.

Nathaniel tied his horse to the wood railing outside the tavern
after riding for a half hour from his cabin nestled in the woods near
the Nissequoque River in the middle of the friendly territory of the
Matinecocks. He knew that Whaleman and Shanghai Jim were inside
since he saw Whaleman's large brown stallion and Shanghai Jim's black
and white piebald tied near the horses of customers.

"Well, if it isn't the Golden Warrior himself," said the obviously
inebriated Whaleman as Nathaniel approached their favorite large oak
table in the right rear corner of the tavern.

"Ah, come on, Whaleman, you're always talking about that
name."

"But, it's still true, isn't it? Why do you object to the name given
to you by Arandel and the great Chief Tackapousha? Tell us again, my
dear friend, about your hair and how you got that special name!"

"Yes, my large, red-headed friend, it was really because of my
blond hair."

"Very yellow blond hair," chirped in Shanghai Jim who was
working on his second large rum. "Whaleman's right. Tell us again. I
always like to hear it. It is really a fantastic story."

When both his friends were sober, they knew that the story
had too many painful memories for Nathaniel, but in their intoxicated
condition, they forgot what they had always been careful to avoid.
Even though Nathaniel knew they were teasing him, it was still difficult
for him to excuse them since the emotional pain was sometimes
intolerable, but fortunately it usually quickly and mercifully subsided.

Whaleman, so called because of his large size, and the

diminutive Shanghai Jim were drinking from pewter mugs filled with rum. Whaleman's favorite meal, hardly touched, was in front of him on the table. The dinner was especially prepared for him by the cook, who originally was from Williamsburg, Virginia – and more specifically, from the reputable and famous King's Arms Tavern. Whaleman's dinner consisted of veal chops with mushrooms, celery, thyme, and Port Wine. Unlike Whaleman, the favorite dish of Nathaniel and Shanghai Jim was Shepherd's Pie, with its mashed potato crust over chopped meat and vegetables.

"Maybe I should call you the 'red-haired warrior' because of that red hair of yours, Whaleman."

"Sounds great to me, Nathaniel. Maybe it'll make me famous like you! Even though I don't think I could be as brave as you were! Maybe I'll also get all those women running after me! All those Indian and white beauties! They might even write a big story like they did about you in Rivington's New York Gazette!"

"It's nothing special, Whaleman. I try not to think about it. Some things should be forgotten."

Nathaniel felt the pain again move from his head to his chest. The sadness was always there ready to assert itself. His usually well-meaning friend continued to forget, in his intoxication, how upset Nathanial would always get when he was reminded of Arandel and why he was called "the Golden Warrior."

Words reminding him of Arandel were bad enough, but those remembrances he couldn't control were everywhere: the scent of a flower, red and yellow colors, a black-haired pretty squaw, someone laughing a certain way. Many times he felt like running and running until he was so exhausted that he would collapse. Whaleman, still not noticing the paleness in Nathaniel's face and his friend's heavy breathing, kept talking.

"That's not what Chief Tackapousha told me, Nathaniel.
He said in 1768 you were a real hero and saved many lives in his
village. If it weren't for you killing all those Connecticut heathens, the
Narragansetts, with your knife and tomahawk…" Suddenly Whaleman
realized what he was saying and that the alcohol had made him forget
how sensitive Nathaniel was about the topic and about Arandel - and he
abruptly became silent for a few seconds.

"God, Nathaniel. I'm sorry. It's the rum talking. I'm sorry.
Forgive me. Sorry."
Shanghai Jim, more sober then Whaleman, tried to change the subject.
"Hey, remember how you used to tell us how you – and we – later
learned to make those dugouts…those canoes like the ones all the
Indians use."

Breathing more normally, and trying to ignore Whaleman's
reference to the Narragansetts, and happy for the change of subject,
Nathaniel spoke slowly. "Yes, as I told you fellows before, in Chief
Tackapousha's village I first learned to make a lot of canoes. We used
to hollow out the trunks of large trees – not the fragile birches – and
burn the bottom. We used to put clay around the bottoms of the trees
so that the fire wouldn't spread. Then we would bring down the trees
with stone axes like we did when we were training to be whalers. Hard
work. Very hard work."

Whaleman, glad that Shanghai Jim had seemingly snapped
Nathaniel out of his momentary sadness, laughed. "That's probably
where you got all those muscles, Nathaniel. Six foot-two, muscles,
blond hair, blue eyes – no wonder you're so popular with the ladies!"

"Too bad I can't be like Nathaniel," said Shanghai Jim. "I can't
help it if I look different – short, and with an odd-looking face that
doesn't seem to belong in this land. If I were in Shanghai, things would
be different. I could get all the women I wanted – tall, short, pretty,

ugly, Chinese, Japanese, Russian. I was like a king over there, and I wasn't even twenty years old. Not like here!"

"You can't even get the few available Indian squaws here?" asked Whaleman.

"Not even them – as you know, my chubby friend. They and the white prostitutes look the other way or they laugh at me. The squaws think I don't know what insults they are saying about me. Besides, there aren't too many squaws who fool around!"

"What do they say, my Chinese friend?" asked Whaleman deciding – as was his usual want – to continue to tease Shanghai.

"The squaws say I'm a 'puny little thing' and 'so ugly.'" Shanghai shook his head. "And the Indian prostitutes, and, as I said, there aren't too many of them, wanted to charge me three times as much!"

Nathaniel knew it was unusual, practically unheard of, for an Indian squaw to become a prostitute. Shanghai Jim, as was his habit, may have been bragging or fantasizing – any squaw who violated the high Indian moral code would be subject to immediate exile. It was too extreme a punishment for a transgressing squaw to abandon the highly valued safety, morality, and culture of her tribe.

It was getting late, and even though he appreciated the conversation with his friends, he was tired from the day's events. The tavern environment always seemed to relax him - the wood floors, split log walls, the long bar's swinging doors at each end, and the dim light provided by candles and whale oil. On the wide shelves behind the bartender, a roly-poly Dutchman, were small kegs of beer and cider and bottles containing various spirits, including whiskey, wine, and rum.

Nathaniel guessed that as soon as he left, his two rum-liking friends would probably retire to the back room where a half-dozen usually nude or semi – nude English and Dutch ladies, for a reasonable charge, would provide sexual gratification also for regular local customers and itinerants. The young women, despite Nathaniel's strong but futile dissent, were hired to please customers and thereby increase the tavern's profit.

CHAPTER 5
JESSIE

Jonathan lately had been thinking of how alike Arandel and Jessie were. They were each five feet, eight inches tall, very attractive, blue-eyed, slim, lithe, and full-breasted. If it weren't for Arandel's medium-length black hair and brownish skin contrasting sharply with Jessie's brown curly hair and white complexion, they could almost, but not quite, be taken for sisters.

Arandel and Jessie had met frequently during their teen-age years in the mid – 1760's when Jessie's father, a businessman, visited Chief Tackapousha's camp for trading purposes. The Chief would exchange such items as Indian-made dugouts and whaling lances and harpoons for manufactured products such as pots, pans, and children's toys imported primarily from England and the Netherlands.

Jessie's father, Morgan, would sometimes take the three young people on "oyster farming" or excursions gathering the valuable oysters along the northern coastal shores of Long Island. Morgan used to say, "I like to have you come along, Nathaniel, because you bring me good luck. Every time we go searching for oysters, we find a rich bed! That's where the money is – oystering and whaling!" Nathaniel would smile, and the two girls would giggle at the compliment, however exaggerated, paid to their companion.

Nathaniel used to recall these pleasant experiences, but what he liked the best was being alone with Arandel on the many trips they made by canoe on the streams and rivers which criss- crossed the island - waterways which, like many of the members of Indian subtribes, had also begun to disappear, for various reasons, by the early 1800's.

Nathaniel would always be content listening to the sweet, modulated voice of Arandel as she identified and described the many wild flowers – and the animals, sometimes drinking from the edge of the water before seeing their canoe and darting into the woods. Once they saw the unusual sight of a wild turkey and deer drinking a few feet from each other.

"Isn't that amazing, Arrie. A turkey and deer getting along together. It's hard to believe."

"Yes, Nathaniel. They both need water. After that, they'll go their separate ways."

Arandel would alternatively speak in English and Algonquin so that Nathaniel could listen and then speak her native language. When he would mangle a particular Algonquin word, she would smile, tease him gently, and then pronounce the word slowly and correctly.

Many years later, he would talk about Arandel to Jessie who was the only other person to whom he could express his deepest thoughts about her. She knew of his love for Arandel and would always listen with understanding and compassion.

When they met again in 1772, Nathaniel had said, "I'm very glad that we got together again. I seem to always be happy when I'm with you, Jess."

"I'm happy, too, Nathaniel. I always thought about you."

"I know, Jessie. It took me a long time to sort things out. I regret not seeing you sooner – there were so many things I wanted to say, but…"

"I understand, Nathaniel. It was very difficult losing Arandel. I know how much you loved her."

"Yes, and you know…you know that I love you, too, Jessie – there, I said it. I didn't know how I would get the courage to tell you…"

Overjoyed, Jessie said, "I love you too, Nathaniel. I've been waiting a long time, longing to hear those words."

She kissed him and started to cry. "I'm so happy, Nathaniel. It's been so long. I think I started to love you when we all went on those oyster hunts with my father years ago. I was so jealous of Arandel, but I saw how much, even at that young age, how you admired and loved her."

"I'm sorry that I didn't speak up sooner, Jessie. Things were too complicated. But, I'm sure now. I've made my peace with the past, I believe. And before I lose my nerve…I want to…if you won't consider me too bold…I would like to marry you, Jessie. If you'll have me."

It was almost too much for Jessie to hear. Everything she dreamed about had come true in the last few minutes. "Yes, yes, Nathaniel, I will. I will." And in that canoe, in a river which he had travelled also with Arandel so many times, they embraced…

Even then, Nathanial couldn't forget that day when they were both eight years old, and he saw Arandel open the flaps of Chief Tackapousha's large wigwam and look at a trembling and near tears little orphaned boy. Even as he hugged Jessie, he still couldn't help remembering the first time he saw Arandel.

CHAPTER 6

NEW LIFE

He remembered little about his father, Samuel, and his mother, Hannah, in the eight years before the attempted Iroquois massacre of the Canarsies in 1758. What else he knew about them had been pieced together in conversations with friends and his mother's parents who both died of natural causes several weeks after the attempted massacre.

Nathaniel's father, a tall and heavyset Englishman, had emigrated in March, 1746, to the New York colony from Southampton in England. On the schooner bound for New York, he had met seventeen-year old, Hannah, a petite blue-eyed blonde. Samuel, usually uncomfortable in the presence of marriageable women, was attracted not only by her shapely figure and beauty, and as he later said, but also by her friendliness and unpretentious manner. The usually taciturn Samuel had felt comfortable telling her about his plans to become a trapper and trader somewhere in the colonies. No woman had previously paid much attention to him let alone to his ambitions except the exuberant and attentive young Hannah.

Encouraged by her sincere interest, he spent many hours on the voyage telling her about his past life. After the recent death of both his parents, he survived by assuaging his sadness by working at various minor jobs in Liverpool.

"My life," he told Hannah, "took a radical turn, even though I didn't realize it at the time. When my cousin, Oliver, returned to England in 1745 after spending five years in the colonies, he told me that he had made a fortune there."

"Doing what, Mr. Townsend…er…may I call you Samuel?"

"Yes. Of course. Please do. To answer your question – he was a fur trapper. He told me an amazing story about the enormous amount of money to be made in the colonies by trapping the wild forest animals and then selling their furs or skins. He said that there was an unbelievable demand for the furs of various animals like beavers, bears, foxes, racoons, and the like. Even the skins of deer and also deer meat, called venison, were easily sold. My cousin Oliver said that he became a very rich man!"

"Is that why you're here, Samuel? Because Oliver said you could get rich like him in the colonies?"

"Yes. But I also thought I needed a change in my life - with maybe an adventure thrown in. A new start."

"I know what you mean. My parents – and I – feel the same way. We heard so much about the New World."

Samuel's optimism may not have been so strong if he knew that Oliver, in order to arouse Samuel's ambition and possibly lessen the grief over the death of his parents, had painted a profitable but incomplete picture of the opportunities in the New World. Oliver deliberately omitted mentioning the hard work involved, the danger of trapping in Indian- occupied land, such as the upper Hudson Valley, where the Mohawks, a subtribe of the Iroquois, could be unpredictable and, therefore, dangerous. Even in dealing with the Mohicans in far western New York colony, if a trapper ventured that far, it could involve some danger as some new farmers were finding out. Samuel had remembered that Oliver had said that he made his fortune trapping along the long Mohawk River which spilled into the Hudson River about a hundred miles north of the large village of New York, sometimes still called New Amsterdam.

Oliver also did not mention that, in addition to the threat of dealing with the volatile upper Hudson Valley Mohawks, the territory abounded with villains – such as thieves who specialized in stealing the accumulated pelts of trappers. Robbers would ambush unsuspecting victims and relieve them not only of furs but also other valuables, including clothing, money, and jewelry, and sometimes their lives.

Trappers travelling by canoe or schooner up or down the Hudson River, if they decided to hunt and trap in the highly desirable environs of the northern area of the New York colony, could be subject to piratical white men with guns or Indians armed with long knives, tomahawks, as well as bows and arrows. Many trappers, faced with such threats, were either too fearful or helpless to ward off the attackers. Oliver himself, with his partner in the northern territory of the New York Colony, had been accosted by a drunken Mohawk Brave, armed with a tomahawk, demanding liquor, wampum, or anything that they possessed. Fortunately, Oliver's partner was able to kill the Brave with one shot from his pistol.

As Samuel had talked to Hannah, he recalled Oliver's optimistic words: "Samuel, it'll make you a new man – and a rich one. You won't have to worry about having enough money to buy food or pay for lodgings. You don't have to count twelve pence to see if you have a shilling. Those days will be gone! And what you have to look forward to! A land of natural beauty – forests filled with colorful wild flowers and roaming animals – ready to be trapped - and trees that reach toward the sky with birds of different sizes and colors perched on the branches and the tree tops."

"You seem to be describing some kind of paradise, Oliver."

"Well, you'll have to see it for yourself, Samuel. There's nothing like it!"

"Probably, Oliver, but I'm not as strong or as daring as you are. I have trouble even deciding whether to journey to London or not. Imagine my going to the New World!"

"You can do it. You forget, Samuel, how shy and timid I was. Like you, I was afraid of doing new things. But I took a chance, and look what happened! I'm not only rich but more confident and not afraid to try anything now. If I can succeed, you certainly can. You're the one who always had the brains, but you seem never to want to use them."

"Thanks for the compliment, Oliver, but..."

"But nothing. Another thing. I see that a good-looking chap like you has no woman in his life. You were always the shy one... which I could never understand. In the colonies there are so many comely and unattached women that you can have your choice: English, Dutch, German, Irish – and if you're willing, perhaps even some young beautiful Indian squaws. Believe me, I've had my fill! And you're not getting any younger. How old are you Samuel? Twenty-seven, twenty-eight?"

"I'm twenty-seven."

"Tell me, Samuel, when's the last time you had a woman? If you don't mind my asking."

"Well, er...actually...actually..."

"Just what I thought," said Oliver, noticing Samuel's hesitation and reddened face. "You better start living, Samuel, before it's too late."

For many weeks, Samuel pondered Oliver's words and tried to imagine himself as a newcomer – a pioneer – in the colonies. When he saw that Oliver, an almost penniless London scrivener six years ago, was now able to buy various businesses and properties and host lavish parties, his cousin's advice seemed more attractive and convincing. What clinched Samuel's decision to change his life and go to what his cousin Oliver described as "paradise" occurred when Oliver offered to pay not only for the passage by schooner to the New World but also for all of the necessary equipment needed by a fur trapper.

On a cold day in March, 1746, Samuel Townsend departed from the port of Southampton, with two large suitcases, and hope for a better life.

CHAPTER 7
APPRENTICE

Samuel became a full-fledged trapper after intensive training in April and May of 1746, with the veteran William Huggins. After working for twenty-two years in Virginia and neighboring colonies, Huggins for the past eight years had been trapping in what originally was new territory for him – the Catskills region in the Upper Hudson Valley adjacent to the winding Mohawk River below Lake Ontario. Huggins, a sixty-year old kindly man, eventually taught Samuel almost all that he himself had learned in his thirty years of trapping animals and selling their furs and skins to eager buyers in New York town and elsewhere.

After disembarking ship in New York Harbor, Samuel had presented Oliver's letter of recommendation to Huggins. Impressed with what Oliver had written, he immediately hired Samuel on a trial basis to replace a youngster who proved that he was ill-fitted by attitude, temperament, and ability for the job. Huggins, a friend of Oliver's former partner, began Samuel's apprenticeship by discussing the skills involved and then showing him specifically how to use the various weapons and trapping devices.

After a few weeks, Huggins was impressed with Samuel's determination and quickness in learning. Huggins had first described safety measures and then the types of simple traps that would be used, including cage traps and padded leg and body traps. Huggins had once used bear traps with teeth, but he considered them so brutal and inhumane that he decided to use them rarely and, even then, reluctantly. Other weapons, used in appropriate and necessary circumstances, were the musket, pistol, rifle, tomahawk, and bow and arrow.

Other aspects of the training sessions included learning how to navigate a canoe on the Hudson River and, if necessary, how to carry the canoe over land, and then hide it. Huggins had also discussed many bits of knowledge learned in his three decades of fur trading and trapping. For example, Samuel was told that bears, for their skins and meat, were in great demand in the thirteen colonies and in Europe. Also, the equally popular but elusive beavers, known to be good swimmers, sometimes by habit or an attempt to evade capture, would remain under water for as long as fifteen minutes. With patience, the hunter could outwait the beaver before snaring it.

"Why are beaver pelts so much in demand?" asked Samuel once.

"They're used for a lot of things, like pelt hats. The soft beaver underbelly has tiny barbs that help keep the material tightly fastened."

"Interesting, Mr. Huggins. I never would have realized that." Samuel, knowing that the Upper Hudson Valley and even further north were rich havens for wild animals, wondered why they couldn't travel a few more miles into Canada.

"Well, Samuel, for a long time the territory in southeastern Canada has been claimed by the hostile and competitive French trappers there. The Indians, a demanding group, permit the French to hunt there if they reimbursed them generously for the privilege. In or near that area are some peaceful but also some very hostile transplanted Iroquois - called Mohawks - and also members of the

Huron, Illinois, and Ottawa clans. Very unfriendly natives! We wouldn't have enough liquor, tobacco, or metal items to give them, let alone carry them there. It's too dangerous a proposition. One Frenchman that I met a few years back near the border said the French had to give the Canadian Indians such things as knives, coffee kettles, axes, blankets, and, sometimes, many trinkets. You had to have these things on hand in order to bribe the Canadian Indians for passage through their land and for trapping there. It's not worth the effort, the expense – and especially the danger!"

"Sounds like good enough reasons for me, Mr. Huggins."

You make me feel like an old man when you still call me Mr. Huggins. Call me William or Bill, Samuel, now that we are friends and partners!"

"Ok, William."

The last things Samuel learned concerned the division of profits and how to carry certain and sufficient kinds of food and, more importantly, how to live off the land. In the forests and in the plains were all kinds of berry bushes and fruit trees and plenty of fish in the streams and rivers. They could also cook and eat some of the game they caught.

"They usually are so many fish inland that you can just about grab them out of the water, Samuel. You won't believe it, but my previous partner and I just about every night, from the rivers, streams, and lakes, caught bass, trout, catfish, and the spiny – plated sturgeon for supper. The sturgeons were so big we could get two or three meals out of them! Even the Hudson River provides fish for the settlers and Indian Tribes."

"Hard to believe, William. Good thing you'll do most of the cooking using the few metal pots, pans, cups, and plates you brought. We don't have to worry about water or firewood, which will be plentiful in the woods. The sulfur matches we have. And since you're doing the cooking, I'll pick the berries and the fruit and try to grab a couple of fish. Sounds so easy, but it probably isn't!"

The next morning, in June of 1746, they started their journey up the Hudson River with the second or trailing large canoe holding traps and various supplies, including non - perishable food. It was faster and less dangerous, Huggins had explained, than traveling north by horse and wagon over difficult terrain and through potentially hostile Iroquois territory. Huggins also distrusted traveling on the 75 – foot long, single mast, Hudson River sloop which usually contained some men of dubious character such as thieves preying on trappers and other passengers.

CHAPTER 8
UP RIVER

After Huggins had been completely satisfied that Samuel was ready to be a professional trapper and trader, he had reviewed with him the route they would take to reach the Upper Hudson Valley region before proceeding westward along the southern side of the Mohawk River. Huggins expected to spend the rest of 1746 and perhaps a few weeks in 1747, for trapping, weather permitting.

They would take turns paddling their lead canoe for the more than the hundred mile journey up the Hudson River which would extend for another 215 miles further north to the headwaters in the Adirondack Mountains. Huggins said that civilization as they knew it would seem to be left behind the further north they went. Huggins added that they would be entering a land with fewer white settlers and more brown-skinned Mohawk Indians, a subtribe of the Iroquois. As Huggins had explained, they would stop about every ten or fifteen miles and moor at waterside supply shacks not only to rest but also to replenish, if necessary, their fresh water supply and food.

Whether it was his fantasizing, or not, Samuel thought that beginning at dusk he heard the sound of drums and that he saw shadowy figures darting in and out of the brush on shore. At night he would see bursts of fire, which would briefly illuminate the sky.

"Oh," responded Huggins to his question, "they're probably campfires of settlers, trappers, or the Mohawks. The Indians also cook outside the wigwams or their small lodges during the warm weather. You hear all sorts of noises – the cries of animals, the whoops of the redmen, and the beat of their drums in ritualistic celebrations. The Mohawks would seize any opportunity to have a reason to drink liquor, dress up, and engage in century-old native dances. Also, there are more and more businessmen looking for iron deposits and other resources south of the Mohawk River. And, there are more loggers and farmers. Times are changing." No matter what Huggins said, Samuel still found it difficult to dispel his growing fears about an environment so frightening and foreign to what he was used to in England.

"I have to admit, William, that this paddling is harder than I thought it would be. And, we still have a long way to go."

"We'll get there soon. Don't worry. What with our taking turns and stopping every ten miles or so, we'll make it and survive all right. It's better than going by wagon or the river sloop! I've done it for many years, and you get used to it. The first time on the river is always rough. Good thing the river flows both ways. And anyway, I am used to the contrary currents on this river. The river and I now are old friends."

Just then, from a distance came the faint sound of galloping horses and loud Indian chants. Noticing the look of concern on Samuel's face, Huggins said, "That's probably some hunting party. Sometimes the Indians yell to scare the bears or deer, or whatever it might be, into an ambush, for easy capture." Sometimes, Huggins didn't add, it could be renegade or vengeful Indians occasionally attacking other Indians or white settlers because of some dispute or to steal livestock or other valuables.

When they approached their landing point above and west of

Albany, Huggins paddled the canoe into a small cove. They dragged and then concealed, with some difficulty, the two large dugout canoes in some heavy brush about fifty yards from shore.

"We'll take a few traps we can carry and a couple of knives and pistols in case we need them. If necessary, we can always come back for muskets, tomahawks, and even bows and arrows. But I doubt if we'll need them. What usually traps the critters are traps. It's only a mile or so to the rich hunting grounds. We'll have to make a few trips back and forth to store the game in our canoes. I've been here before, Samuel. It's a good and safe place here to hide the canoes and furs in them. In fact, if we're lucky, we should come across a lot of beavers in a nearby stream. You're on your way, Samuel, to becoming a rich man!"

As they walked toward what seemed to be an unusually deep stream, Samuel said, "Tell me again, William, who'll buy the furs and skins, and how much can we sell them for?"

"We have two options. We can sell them at the Fort Orange Dutch trading post a mile north of Albany. It's pretty close to here. The Dutch, who first settled in this area, still call it Fort Orange, which was the Dutch name for Albany before 1644 when the British captured it. Or we can haul them south to New York where we'll get a better price. My previous partner and I used to trap a few more dozen beavers and racoons to make up for the less money we would get for selling them at Fort Orange and not in New York town. It was much easier that way. We didn't have to be bothered with transporting the furs and skins a long distance down river to New York and worry about robbers coming from the shore. It's easier carrying money than to transport all those furs. We got robbed once, my first time trapping in Virginia, and it was the last time. Fortunately we didn't have much because we had just started trapping. It was still a terrible feeling!"

Huggins thought for a while and then continued his explanation. "The buying price for furs has gone down a bit because of the French in Canada and the Russians flooding the European market with them. The French also sell a lot of furs in the colonies. But, we can still make a handsome profit which should suit you, my English friend. For example, the Dutchmen at the trading post will give us, depending on the demand, anywhere from 6 to 9 guilders per fur. A guilder, as I may have told you, is equal to two of your English shillings. Six guilders, maybe more, per beaver pelt, would be worth at least twelve shillings. Multiply that by the hundreds of beavers, and I expect we'll also get many more guilders for the bear and deer skins, which are also very popular and much in demand, and we'll end up with a lot of money! Figure in the other assorted furs and skins and even some skins or feathers of the foxes, opossums, racoons, turkeys, wolves, and a bunch of those other critters. We might have so many furs that we'll have to make two trips to Fort Orange! But, we'll see. You could end up with enough money to buy half of London, Samuel!"

"I don't think it'll be enough to buy half of London, but what you said really excites me. I can do a lot of things with all that money. Buy a house in or near London, buy or start a business or two, and even be an investor. Hard to believe, William!"

"Maybe you might even get married, Samuel! I'm surprised a strapping, good appearing young fellow like you hasn't yet married! "If the London lasses find out you have so much money, you'll be married before you know it!" Huggins laughed. "I invested my money in land and a couple of businesses and have some cash stored away. Before you ask, yes, I've been married a couple of times, but they couldn't take being alone so much when I was on these hunting trips. But who knows…maybe…"

"Another concern, William. I heard the Iroquois, or Mohawks

as they're called up here, can be very unpredictable and sometimes dangerous. Is that true?"

"There are a few that get ornery, especially in the late winter when there's less hunting and fishing and when they feel isolated by the snow. They are like the Narragansetts in Connecticut who, when they really run low on food or possessions, exact tribute from weaker tribes. Since they're all Mohawks up here, they usually don't attack each other for tribute. There are petty internal arguments but nothing really serious. Give them some wampum or trinkets or liquor, and the Mohawks will be happy."

"Wampum is still used by the Indians up here?"

"Yes, Samuel, but not as much. The Mohawks collect shells from along the Mohawk and Hudson Rivers. They like to trade, and some still use the sea shells as money. Black beads or shells are considered more valuable than white ones. The Mohawks are always trading one thing for another. The English, as you know, use shillings or pence, the Dutch guilders or stuyvers, and the Indians have their wampum. What may be a big problem is that the Indians do not accept artificial or non-natural wampum, which the Dutch are starting to transport to the colonies. Hard to tell which shells or beads are real and which aren't. Could be trouble. But, as I said before, times are changing. Wampum is starting to give way to English money or colonial paper and coins."

"William, I get a history lesson just listening to you."

"You'd know a lot more, too, if you've been here as long as I have."

"I doubt if I will. I don't think I'll be here that long to know that much or even get married! Maybe…maybe in England. I don't know. Maybe. It could happen, I guess. We'll see."

Both of them worked very hard, trapping not only south of the

Mohawk River and below Lake Ontario but also venturing an additional
two miles further west of the Hudson River. A few miles further west
and they would have entered Mohican territory which Higgins preferred
not to do. A week later Huggins said, "Samuel, we've got so many pelts
I can't believe it! I've never been so lucky before and in such a short
period of time! There's a fortune in the furs piled in our two canoes.
We'll hardly be able to fit in the boats ourselves! No wonder some
trappers refer to furs as 'soft gold.' We'll be rich just with the beaver,
raccoon, some moose, and the hard to get fox pelts! That doesn't
even include the skins of the bear, deer, and the wolves, which I like to
call 'howlers!' The trading post will love the deer so they can sell the
venison and also its antlers, which the white folk and Mohawks can use
for tools and arrow tips. The Mohawks make clothes out of bear skins
and also clubs out of bear bones, which the Iroquois and Algonquins
down south prefer to call tomahawks. Both put a metal or bone axe at
the tip. Deadly weapons!"

"What about the other smaller furs and skins we have?" asked
Samuel.

"You mean like the muskrats, rabbits, and squirrels? They'll
bring in some guilders, too. If we have no room, we can bundle them
up and drag them in those water-proof strong sacks we bought and
which we can tie to the back of both boats. We probably could have
used a third canoe! But it's only about a couple of miles up river to the
Dutch trading post. I doubt if the fish up here will get to them because
the special sacks are pretty heavy, water proof, and thick. I don't think
we'll make another trip to Fort Orange since I think we've got quite a
haul here, Samuel."

"I guess the Indians and settlers like the meat of birds,
opossum, squirrels, and the like, William. I'd get sick eating that kind
of food. In England I got used to beef, chicken, mutton, pork, and veal

plus vegetables like beans, carrots, and peas. The one English meal they have here that I like is Shepherd's Pie – a really delicious meat and vegetable pie with a mashed potato crust. At least one thing reminds me of England!"

After an unseasonable stretch of warm winter, on this particular day, in late November, 1746, several days before they were to head for the Fort Orange trading post and then paddle south on the Hudson River to New York, Samuel felt an unaccountable feeling of dread. Was it because of the sudden arrival of coldness and a bitter wind blowing inland from the Hudson River, and the few early snowflakes falling aimlessly to the ground?

CHAPTER 9
A STRING OF BEADS

Samuel looked up at the darkening sky, and the feeling of foreboding
again swept over him. What was there to worry about, he thought.
Very soon he would be a rich man and only after one short season of
trapping. Huggins told him that such a surprising wealth of furs usually
was the result of almost a year's work. He could return to London – or
wherever he wanted – and live the luxurious life style of an English
gentleman.

First, they had to exchange the furs for English pound sterling.
At the rate of 20 shillings per one pound sterling, he and William
would certainly be rich men. With this expectation, he would savor
the arduous trip back to New York not with a feeling of uncertainty and
anxiety, but with contentment. The prospect of returning as a wealthy
man to the comfort and security of his room in the Kings Arms Inn in
the town of New York made him very joyful.

What caused the unexpected misfortune was not illness, a snow
storm, or an attack by the Mohawks. It started innocently enough with
the negotiations for a sale of a simple strand of wampum beads to a
Mohawk Brave.

Huggins in New York unknowingly had bought a large number
of artificial wampum beads and beaded belts to be used to trade for

furs with the Mohawk Indians. The Dutch seller in the city was intent on making a quick sale and falsely told Huggins that "These are genuine wampum, good wherever there are Indians." It was difficult for some people to distinguish the false beads from the genuine. In the late 1740's, the use of Indian wampum was still used but was increasingly being replaced by standard English currency, colonial coins, the newly printed colonial paper money, and to some extent, Dutch money. But some Indians in the New York colony still preferred wampum – the real white and even more valuable black sea shells.

On that last day in November, when they were close to leaving in case the sudden very light snowfall became too heavy, they were approached by a seemingly friendly Mohawk Brave, wearing in his hair the traditional eagle feathers, who offered twenty beaver pelts in exchange for equivalent wampum.

On an impulse, the Brave, after saying "she – kon" (greetings), asked if Huggins by chance had one of the genuine belts called "Hiawatha Belts." The few special belts still in existence were considered sacred by the Iroquois because they symbolized the treaty and unity of the "Five Nations of the Iroquois." The five nations were Cayuga, Mohawk, Oneida, Onondaga, and Seneca subtribes. The belt consisted of white hearts separated by white squares.

It was unfortunate that of the 15,000 Iroquois, including Mohawks, in the New York colony, he was one of the few Indians who could tell whether the special belt was genuine or fake. When Huggins gave him the belt, which the Brave curiously and intently examined, Huggins felt he was going to make one last profitable transaction.

Suddenly the Brave let out a piercing cry and threw the fake belt to the ground. Hearing the Brave spew a string of heated words, Huggins, not understanding the angry curses, assumed he was dissatisfied with the belt, for some reason. He reached into his large canvas bag to find some trinkets or beads which he thought would appease the tall, fierce-looking warrior. "I'll give him something that'll satisfy him and make him happy," said Huggins as he searched deeper in his bag.

The Mohawk, in his fury at being offered a false sacred belt in exchange for his many valuable beaver furs, misinterpreted Huggins' actions as an attempt to look for a weapon. With a swift motion that Samuel later said seemed like a surreal image, the Indian had removed his tomahawk from underneath his snakeskin belt holding up his leggings and swung it at the head of the unsuspecting Huggins as Samuel watched in shock. Stunned and frozen in fear and disbelief, Samuel couldn't immediately process what had just happened. After he looked down at the lifeless Huggins, he realized that the murderous, large Mohawk was coming at him with the tomahawk still in his hand.

CHAPTER 10
NOT A DREAM

Decades later, Samuel still could not completely erase from his memory that dreadful scene of Huggins lying dead on the ground and the Mohawk warrior furiously charging at him and swinging his tomahawk. It was difficult for him to look back and think that such a grotesque scene could occur in what was a deceptively peaceful woodland setting, with snow lightly descending on the trees and ground.

Samuel would sometimes wake up at night and reach for an imaginary dagger after dreaming about the tall Mohawk Brave dressed in winter leggings, deerskin jacket, and above - ankle boots.

He still found it remarkable that he could remember exactly what the Indian was wearing on that late November day in 1746 and that he had the presence of mind then to defend himself. Even though his defensive reaction had been played in slow motion so many times in his dreams and waking moments, he was still amazed at what he had done. He had quickly removed his long hunting knife from its sheath and tried nervously and clumsily to grip it by its handle. In desperation, he hurled the knife, not by the handle but with his hand on the sharp side of the blade, at the charging Mohawk. As luck would have it, the quickly but awkwardly released blade struck the Brave fatally in the chest. Samuel later said that luck had smiled on him for the second time. He and William had been unbelievably successful in collecting hundreds of pelts and skins, and Samuel's good fortune had continued with his bizarre killing of a frenzied Mohawk who was intent on doing to him what he had just done to Huggins.

As Samuel, still shaking, kneeled on the wet ground, and sobbed at the sight of his dead friend and partner. Saying a prayer for Huggins and to God for enabling him to survive, he vowed never again to kill any living thing – man or animal.

After grieving for most of the day, he debated what to do with all of the furs and skins. He decided to follow William's practical plan to sell the furs to the Dutch at the nearby trading post instead of dangerously transporting them alone many miles down river to New York. He remembered what Huggins had told him about many fur traders paddling down the Hudson River being intercepted and robbed not only by renegade Indians, but by what Huggins called "white river pirates."

Samuel rowed east down the last stretch of the 143 mile long eastward flowing Mohawk River and then turned north on the Hudson River toward the trading post. At the Dutch trading post, as predicted by Huggins, he was paid a reasonable amount for each kind of fur or skin as per market demand with beaver fur being the most profitable. In order to make his down river journey as easy as possible, he sold the second canoe. The profits, mostly in English and Dutch paper currency, were strapped inside a water-proof money belt that he bought at the trading post after he had sold the furs. The loose coins, including the recently minted coarse colonial copper coins, were put in a leather pouch attached to the money belt strapped securely around his waist.

Samuel untied the lead canoe from the wharf in the front of the trading post and then rowed west through the short inlet before heading south down the Hudson River. The light snowfall had stopped and been replaced again by mild weather which would help make his journey less arduous. The prospect, however, of travelling alone on the return trip terrified him. Samuel tried to imagine what Huggins would tell him to do if he were there, sitting beside him, smiling, and telling tales of trapping in the very early days. He wiped the tears from his eyes.

CHAPTER 11
DOWN RIVER

Exhausted after rowing only three miles down the Hudson River, he stopped at a food shack to rest, buy some bottled and hopefully fresh spring water, and particularly to talk to someone – anyone – to validate his feeling of normality and to try to forget the horror of what had happened. He hadn't eaten that morning so he bought some smoked venison and hard biscuits. The hardtack was a bit too hard, but in his hunger he didn't mind.

After resuming his journey, he noted that in the few months they had been trapping up north, some more food shacks and trading posts had sprung up along the river. As Huggins had told him, the southern half of the three hundred and fifteen mile long Hudson River had alternating low and high tides. The technical explanation had confused him, but Samuel knew that moving with a high tide, which seemed now to be the case, would make it easier for him to row and eventually reach his destination.

Huggins had also mentioned that the Hudson River, like the East River, in certain places up river and down river, had very swift moving currents, which could move as fast as four knots. Such unpredictable currents could upset canoes and even some larger vessels unless they were anticipated and handled by experienced boatmen.

Huggins had been going up and down the Hudson River for many years and through personal experience, and questioning of his river pilot friends, he had become very skillful in navigating the river. Huggins had also said many times that he disliked traveling on the commercial river sloops, which contained too many men with ulterior motives. Some thieves noted where trappers landed and followed them to steal the results of their labor, and in some cases, injure or kill them. In the early days, especially, it was thus dangerous to transport furs on the few north or south bound Hudson River sloops since many a trapper had been thrown overboard after being robbed of his money or furs or both, which he had collected after months of hard work. It was an easy way for scheming and unconscionable thieves to steal money or furs with hardly any effort. Thus, Huggins soon learned to become a very guarded and suspicious man and trusted no one except himself and his carefully selected partners.

Also, in the 1600's and early1700's, there had been much game just north of the town of New York, but the steady influx of trappers, mostly Dutch and English, and the expansion of settlements tended to decimate radically the number of wild animals, especially beavers, bears, and deer, in that region. Trappers, to find enough game, were then forced to go further and further north toward the Upper Hudson Valley and Mohawk territory or risk much danger by going even further into Canada where hostile Indians ruled.

That first moonlit night, alone with his thoughts and being overly sensitive to even the slightest suspicious sound, he tried to get some sleep. The task of rowing northward had been much easier when he and Huggins had alternated shifts. Samuel hoped that in the few minutes that he might be able to sleep, the current would unerringly move the canoe down river. If he couldn't sleep or if there were some other problem, he would have to row to shore, hide the large dugout canoe among the coastal shrubbery, and try to sleep until the morning.

After dozing for a while, Samuel woke up disoriented and found that his canoe had been carried sideways until it bumped and floundered against the edge of the western side of the river. Panicking, he imagined that not only all sorts of noises were coming from the nearby woods but also that someone, perhaps an Indian, would suddenly come out of the darkness and attack him.

Using his oar, he pushed away from the shore, grabbed the other oar, and rowed as fast as he could until he once more was, he thought, safely in the middle of the river. Even with no snow and mild weather and a soft, cool breeze coming from the west, he was sweating and continually had to wipe the perspiration from his face and eyes and the fear from his mind.

CHAPTER 12
NIGHT HORROR

Despite his fears, Samuel felt more secure and confident in the isolation of the darkness than he did rowing in daylight. He was grateful that Huggins had purchased such a well-built dugout canoe from an Algonquin tribe in Canarsies Town across the East River on Long Island. The canoe, because it was made from the soft white wood of the tulip tree, was lighter, surprisingly more durable and easier to maneuver, than the birch or elm wood canoe usually made by the Iroquois and New England tribes.

Reminiscing in the middle of the next evening at twice being favored by the capricious "Lady Luck," he suddenly heard the churning of oars coming from the starboard side. Peering frantically in the moonless night, he suddenly realized that a canoe was moving quickly toward him. When the boat was just a few yards away, he saw an Indian stop rowing and take out a tomahawk. Samuel remembered Huggins' accounts of Indians and white men intercepting and robbing trappers up and down the Hudson River. Samuel later said that if he hadn't spotted the Indian, he probably would have been killed or thrown alive overboard and faced with trying to swim to shore, which was more than a hundred yards away.

As the Brave raised his tomahawk, Samuel removed an oar

from the U-shaped oarlock and swung it at the Indian's head. Stunned by the unexpected blow from a man he thought was sleeping, unaware, or inattentive, the Brave was knocked unconscious into the water and then swiftly carried away by the surging current. Shocked at what had just happened, he struggled for a few moments to breathe normally. Regaining his composure, he pushed the attacker's boat away, looked cautiously around him, and continued rowing south. For the third time, he thought, luck had been on his side.

When the trauma had completely left him, he tried to assess how differently his life had changed – from a quiet, mild Englishman working at mundane jobs in Liverpool to trapping in the "New World," a land of pioneers, Indians, and woodland beauty – loveliness where he had ironically almost lost his life.

Travelling up and down the Hudson by canoe at first seemed to be an exhausting undertaking, but Huggins' explanation that the many currents, moving alternately in both directions, made it much easier than what one would have expected. As Huggins had predicted, the canoe, caught abruptly in a sudden rapid current, was moving south swiftly without the need for Samuel to use the two oars.

Samuel looked at the shoreline on both sides and knew that many of the Iroquois were in settlements close to the river. The Iroquois-dominated territory, from northern New York village to the northern limit of the Upper Hudson Valley, has been compared to the size of the early Roman Empire which existed more than two thousand years ago. Huggins had told him that because the Iroquois were more powerful and better organized than the other tribes, including the Algonquin Nation, the tribute-demanding Iroquois were described as the "Romans of the Indian World." The hierarchal structure of the Iroquois organization had also impressed the British who were actively cultivating the support of the numerous and powerful Iroquois Indians in case there was a confrontation with the colonials.

Samuel could hardly wait to return to his long-term rented lodging at the new King's Arms Inn on the former Anthony Bleeker farm on Manhattan Island. The still mostly underdeveloped area, abounding with many trees – chestnut, oak, pine, and numerous berry bushes – was going to be the future site of many businesses, including another inn and a new fishery. In the late 1740's, this part of southern Manhattan, now called the Battery, lived a few English settlers and some peaceful Algonquins who had wandered for various reasons from Long Island.

Before he reached his destination, he had to leave the Hudson River where it joined the East River. A mile before that, where the river narrowed, he encountered a bizarre scene. Standing at the northern tip of Manhattan Island where boats came as close as fifty yards, there were a few young Indians and white females standing naked and offering their bodies for a small fee or for furs. Behind the nude women were small makeshift shacks with mat beds inside. Apparently the women figured that the men, after months in the wild of the forests, would be starved for female attention and sex. It was an amazing and tempting sight that momentarily held his interest until he remembered his aversion to prostitutes and desire to get to his apartment and try to forget the tragedy which occurred only a few days ago.

After reaching the southern tip of Manhattan, he tied his canoe at the public wharf, and walked the nearly half mile to the inn, almost counting the steps until he could retreat into the safety and refuge of his small room. As he closed the door of his room and then locked it, his emotions welled up as he confronted the full reality of the death of his dear friend William Huggins and his own encounters twice with death.

CHAPTER 13
CANARSIES TOWN

Despite the substantial amount of money he had made after months of hunting, Samuel vowed that he would never return to the business of trapping animals and selling their furs and skins. For several weeks, he debated whether to return to England or to yield to the fascinating lure of pioneer life with all of its new and exciting possibilities.

For the fourth time, he later said, luck had come his way. He had been successful with Huggins, fortunate in killing Huggins' murderer, in warding off a river pirate, and now in meeting Hiram Tyler. In a chance meeting in the King's Arms Inn in July, 1747, he met Hiram Tyler, an acquaintance of Huggins. After offering his sympathy for the macabre death of their mutual friend, Tyler explored Samuel's interest in investing some of his profits in a joint and potentially lucrative business venture.

Samuel listened with much interest as Tyler told him of a New World business opportunity owning a general store, located a mile east of the East River, in Canarsies Town in friendly Canarsie Indian territory on Long Island. The owner, an elderly gentleman, wanted to retire and return to England to "see my folks again before I die." The business, slowly built up over the years as the area prospered with the arrival of new settlers, was making a profit selling a variety of items.

Jabez Brown was the proprietor since 1702 when, with the help of Indians, he built the small store in the heart of a small plain surrounded by woods. Originally selling furs and also tools made from animal bones brought to him by members of the Algonquin subtribes, he gradually added imports manufactured in England and the Netherlands. Jabez sold things that couldn't be made by the Indians, and which were also needed by settlers: pots, pans, farming implements, blankets, and what was called "dressed" (formal or regular) and "undressed" (informal) clothing.

His customers in the area, eventually renamed Brooklyn, included Indians from all the thirteen island Algonquin subtribes, as well as white settlers and various transients. The new settlers needed supplies on their way to build homes, establish farms, or find work in the expanding whaling industry flourishing principally on the north shore of Long Island or "Paumanok" as some Indians still called it. Most of the settlers were newly arrived from England and a few from Germany and the Netherlands. Tyler had learned of Jabez Brown's desire to sell the store through an advertisement in the recently established Rivington's Gazette.

"It's a good business," Jabez had told Tyler. "I spent fifty years building it up. Went through two wives but unfortunately had no children. You can have it at a reasonable price since I made enough money out of it, and I want to go back to England to see my relatives and friends – if any are still alive!"

After being ferried by a large dugout canoe from Manhattan across the East River to examine the store, Tyler had decided to buy the business if he could find a reliable financial partner. What further impressed Tyler was its closeness to the East River, which would expedite the transportation of goods from the city, and also its location amid the incredible natural woodland beauty. Tyler had never seen

such an abundance of flowers, bushes, and trees fringing the edges of
two small streams near the town.

"It's very beautiful there," Tyler told Samuel. "I thought New
York was rustic, but wait till you see what's all around the store!"
Samuel was about to tell him about the scenic environment near the
Mohawk River, but the thought froze in his mind.

After they completed the transaction, with both splitting the
cost, Tyler discussed more of what Jabez had told him about the area's
history and the volume of business during the winter.

"You know, Samuel, this place already has some history to it.
The Canarsies, who had many name changes in the last hundred years,
were the first island Indians to greet the explorer Henry Hudson in
1609. Hudson, who worked for the Dutch East India Company, didn't
know that he had landed on an island in his search for the Northwest
Passage to the Orient."

"Well, at least he gave the river a name," answered Samuel.
"And what did Jabez say our business will be like in the winter?"

"Jabez told me not to worry about the weather. There's not as
much hunting and fishing, obviously, when the snow comes. There's
some business, however. But, if we stock up on our usual goods plus
smoked or dried foods – such as clams, deer meat, and fish – we
should do pretty well." Samuel and Tyler worked well together. In
addition to physically expanding the store, they carefully estimated
future business needs and the calculation of inventory.

"You know, Samuel, that the redskins will sell us things or
barter for what they need. They make and sell us tools – and weapons
– from the deer antlers and other animal bones."

"You call them redskins, Hiram? They are more brown-skinned
than red."

"True, but they look red to me. It's probably those dyes or

paints – or whatever they are – that they smear on their face and body. Seems like they prefer red – as well as black, white, and yellow."

"I don't care how they look, Hiram, as long as they're peaceful, which the Canarsies seem to be."

"Getting back to stock, Samuel. As you know, Jabez told us how to order goods from England and the Netherlands. He gave us his contact in New York and what the current prices are – wholesale, retail. Very exacting fellow Jabez is!"

"What about getting the goods from New York to here in the winter when the East River is frozen?" asked Samuel.

"What he said surprised me. Even though the East River freezes solid in the winter, it can still be crossed – not by boat but by horses and wagons. Anything – light or heavy – can be moved across the thick ice – such as metal objects, furniture, games, toys…anything. Can you believe that! Jabez used to hire men, young boys, or Indians, to transport the goods over the East River, which by the way some settlers still call by its old name – 'Sound River.'"

"I also remember Jabez saying something about black slaves also doing that work. I don't believe in the inhumane practice of the slave trade, Hiram."

"I agree with you. But some of the settlers hire out their black slaves to make more money. Besides, Jabez used very few of them. Only when he was really strapped. We don't have to employ any of them."

"Fine. I understand, Hiram, that in 1726, they started bringing slaves to the Louisiana Territory, and that today there are over 100,000 black slaves in the colonies. Like you, I'd rather not use them. It's unconscionable! As I said, I don't believe in slavery. It's immoral, barbaric."

"OK, Samuel, I understand. Whatever you say. We can hire

enough settlers and Indians. Don't be concerned about it. Getting back to the East River, Jabez said that seamen, over the years, told him some interesting facts."

"Like what?"

"Such as the East River is a tidal strait sixteen miles long and anywhere from 600 to 4,000 feet wide. Our merchandise can be transported at the narrowest point – two hundred yards. Under the ice, the water depth varies from thirty to sixty feet. No one in the winter fell in yet, said Jabez! On another topic, Samuel, merchandise. What would you think about selling artificial wampum – similar to the real valuable black beads and white ones? Jabez said they were recently advertised by his Dutch contact in New York. He was debating whether or not to buy and sell them."

"No, no, we can't sell fake wampum or wampum belts. It's like making false English shillings. It's wrong, dangerous, and fraudulent. The Indians would know they're fake. They would feel deceived. It would cause a lot of serious trouble!"

"Why are you so upset, my friend?"

"They're not real, as I said, Hiram. We can't be responsible for circulating false Indian money, which would upset not only the Indians but also the white settlers." Unable to speak anymore and feeling dizzy, Samuel had to steady himself by leaning on a chair.

"My God, Samuel! Are you all right? What's the matter? I thought you were going to faint!"

"It's OK, Hiram. I'm all right now. I just had to catch my breath. It's what you said about selling the artificial wampum."

For the first time, Samuel then told Hiram in detail what happened to him and Huggins on that wintry day in the woods near the Mohawk River – a tragedy which seemed so long ago. He told about the light snow falling on the russet-colored leaves and the solitude of a glade being broken only by the occasional chirping of a few winter birds. From that day on, Samuel said, he had difficulty not associating woodland beauty with the incongruity of horror and violence.

Chapter 14
Storekeeper

The two partners gradually added to their inventory by asking their customers what they needed and what they preferred to purchase or barter. Because of the growing number of families in the area, food was becoming a favorite purchase. The non-farmer brought fruit, vegetables, and smoked meat as well as utensils for cooking and eating. The Algonquin Indians preferred to barter by exchanging furs, which were getting less available on the island, smoked deer venison, and meat from bears that, like deer, were also gradually becoming less available because of excessive hunting. Such things as deer antlers and other deer bones, which could be fashioned into tools, were thus becoming even more scarce.

Samuel and Hiram also noted that the Chandler, whaler, and oysterman could still provide products that were popular. Whale oil was used for lamps, and whalebone was fashioned into a variety of tools. The whaling industry was booming along the north shore and, to a lesser extent, on the south shore of the island. The Chandler could make large quantities of candles and soap. The abundant oysters also were in great demand.

Candles, particularly, were used by most settlers. Samuel learned that a local housewife, an amateur Chandler, was proficient in making all sorts of candles and soaps. One day he visited her at her cottage, about a half mile east of the store, to arrange for purchase of her candles and soap and to study her methods used in making them. After a preliminary conversation, she demonstrated the process of making candles. She melted meat fat from hogs, cows, or sheep to form hot, solid tallow. Linen wicks, tied to a stick, were dipped many times into the hot, white tallow until the desired candle thickness was achieved.

Later, Hiram complimented his enterprising partner. "Now we don't have to order candles or soap from our New York distributor. It'll cost us less, and therefore we can sell them for less."
In the following year, 1748, they decided also to sell shellfish such as smoked clams, the popular oysters, and scallops. They hired a young man not only to do the fishing for shellfish along the island's shores but also for freshwater fish, such as trout, in the streams and rivers, and to smoke and preserve them. The smoked shellfish and freshwater fish kept well and were usually all sold before the winter ended.

Things were very peaceful in Canarsies Town since the island was barely affected by the French and Indian War which began in 1754. The conflict between British rulers and colonists, however, was slowly increasing, particularly because of British-imposed taxes, but full-fledged war wouldn't occur until almost twenty years later.

Canarsies Town, formed by white settlers more than fifty years before, began to develop rapidly. An Anglican Church was built and was soon followed by businesses which were also common to many of the island's other pioneer towns. Established were an apothecary, blacksmith, Chandler, inn, and a grist mill, and a waterwheel, just outside of town, which facilitated the grinding of grain into flour and the cutting of lumber.

The local inn, a combination tavern and hotel, served

townspeople and transients alike. Many settlers, not only from the west but also from the eastern end of the island, stayed there on their way to or from New York and the Upper Hudson Valley region. Accommodations, however, were not very comfortable. It wasn't unusual for 5 or 6 male strangers to sleep in the same unheated, hot, or un-ventilated room.

Luck, in 1748, would favor Samuel for the fifth time. On a day in early 1748, a day Samuel later said was the luckiest day of his life, he was returning from the apothecary shop where he had been treated for poison ivy with the application on his hands of jewelreed herbs, he thought he recognized the young woman walking toward him. She later said that she immediately recognized him "Why, Mr. Townsend, I can't believe it's you. Here of all places!"

Samuel, surprised but very pleased, shyly replied, "Yes. Yes. I remember. You're Hannah… Hannah Gardiner. We met on the ship coming over. We had some very pleasant conversations as I recall."

"Yes. I remember. I always wondered what happened to you. I didn't have a chance to say good-bye in all that confusion getting off the ship. How long ago was that, Mr. Townsend?"

"Several years ago, I believe. My, you're grown up a bit. If I remember correctly, you were seventeen years old then."

How could Samuel forget the five-feet-eight effervescent teen-ager with blonde hair who made his eight-week journey from Southampton to New York Harbor so pleasurable. In fact, many times in the past, he wondered what had happened to her and how he had regretted not being forward enough on the ship to ask if he could contact her later. As they talked and walked on the wood planks flanking the narrow dirt street which was only wide enough for the passage of a horse and wagon, Samuel's attraction to her was rekindled.

He was determined this time, if she weren't married, to further their relationship. "We had so many good talks. I was sorry not to be able to ask you something before you left the schooner." Samuel was amazed at his uncharacteristic boldness in making such a direct comment. Years before, he would have been too shy and reticent to dare speak that way to a young and unmarried lady.

"I wanted to ask you, Miss Gardiner…"

"Call me Hannah. I feel like we're old friends. And, if you don't mind, I'll call you…"

"Samuel. As you used to. That'll be fine. I also feel like we've known each other for a long time."

"Fine, Samuel. I always liked that name… Samuel."

"And Hannah is a pretty name. But, as I was saying, if you're not engaged…or married…"

"I'm not!"

"Then I would consider it an honor if you would let…let me call on you - with your parent's permission, of course - some day soon."

"I would be delighted, Samuel. I'm sure they would approve. They told me on the ship that you looked like a fine, respectable gentleman."

"I'm happy to hear that."

After more conversation exchanging their histories since they first met, they made plans to meet again on the Sabbath. Two months later, Samuel proposed and, with the blessing of her parents, she accepted. The marriage soon after was a simple affair, attended by just a few close friends, but for Samuel it was the most joyous event of his young life.

Hannah would in late 1748 give birth to twins, Jonathan and Martha. Samuel, however, would never live long enough to know that his son would play such a significant role during the American Revolution when the survival of General George Washington would depend on the bravery of colonial scout and spy, Nathaniel Townsend.

CHAPTER 15
MARRIED LIFE

Hannah and Samuel led very happy and peaceful lives for the next eight years in their cottage located less than a mile north of their General Store.

What endeared her even more to Samuel was his kind invitation for her aged and sickly parents to live with them in their cottage built soon after their marriage. With medical doctors so scarce on the island, Hannah's parents could at least be tended to by their daughter. To show her appreciation for the love and compassion shown by her husband for her parents, Hannah volunteered to assist Samuel and Hiram by working three days a week in the General Store.

"Hannah, you don't have to help us. You have enough to do. Hiram and I, and a young fellow who works part-time, can handle everything."

"I have to help out, Samuel. It's the least I can do."

"The least! Hannah, you get and cook the food, clean the cottage, tend to the vegetable garden, and help your parents. You do enough!"

"I still have time to help. And besides we'll be together more. You leave the cottage most days at six in the morning and come home twelve or thirteen hours later."

"True. But Hiram and I are trying to work out a schedule so we won't have to spend so much time at the store."

"I'm still waiting for that to happen. Please, Samuel. If I work there, I won't miss you so much!"

The last comment was enough to overcome his resistance, and Hannah began working the first three days of the following week. She adjusted quickly to the process of selling and becoming familiar with all the products sold. She was so adept at her job that she even had time to sweep the floor and also chat with her husband.

There was one thing, however, that Samuel noticed that made his wife nervous. "I see you seem to get a little nervous when Indian customers come in. You shouldn't be. The Algonquins are very gentle, respectful people, unlike the occasional Iroquois who come in."

"I know that you have sufficient reason to be fearful of the Iroquois, especially the Mohawk clan, Samuel. But, I have no reason. They just seem to…how can I explain it…frighten me. It's probably just my imagination, or intuition, or something."

"Hannah, if we lived in the 1600's, you might have a reason to be afraid. The Canarsies weren't always so friendly, and there were a lot of internal Indian wars going on then. Especially, the Montauks way out east who then were considered to be the most violent, tribute-demanding tribe on the island. The Montauks came here by canoe via the many streams and rivers and even along the shore of the Sound which they called the "Mighty Bay." Even the Pequots and the Narragansetts from Connecticut in the 1600's used to row south across the Sound and ravage Paumanok Indian villages. But, things are more peaceful here, now."

"Who are the Montauks, Samuel? I don't hear too much about them."

"As I said, they used to have a pretty brutal history almost a hundred years ago. Montauk means 'fortified place' in Algonquin. Chief Wyandanch, then their powerful and famous sachem, or chieftain, protected his people by building a fort around their settlement."

"You know a lot about the history of Indians, around here, my wonderful, handsome husband."

"Well, thank you Hannah, for the compliment. And, I would like you to know that I always thought you were very beautiful ever since we met on the ship."

"I know, Samuel. I think you could call it a mutual attraction."

"And also," continued Samuel, with his face blushing, "I hear a lot of white settlers and Indians talking about their history. Some of the Indians seemed to have learned English very quickly. That's how I learned that the Montauks, way out east, who control, or should I say inhabit there, the land east and north to the Atlantic Ocean, and also what's called Gardiner's Island."

"Gardiner's Island. Was there a person named Gardiner? Maybe I'm related to him."

"I doubt it, Hannah. I don't think your ancestors were around here in the 1600's. Or were they?"

"No. I doubt it. It can't be, Samuel."

"Gardiner, Hannah, was a white settler who because he befriended Chief Wyandanch, helped ease tensions in the area between the white settlers and the Montauks. Despite Gardiner's efforts, however, the very powerful Montauks continued to exact tributes, such as wampum, food, and even Indian squaws, from many island tribes, including the Canarsies. Gardiner who, I think, must have been a very peaceful man and quite heroic, eventually retired to the nearby island named after him."

"I wish I was related to him, Samuel. Since I like the 'peaceful and heroic' part."

"Could be, you're related to him," said Samuel, smiling. "But, very unlikely. I'll tell you one thing. The old Montauks in the 1600's remind me of the Mohawk tribe up near Canada. I know you can't judge them all by one murderous Mohawk...but..."

"You have to forget the past, Samuel. It's over and done with. The past is the past. You can't change it."

"Hannah. I try but I can't seem to forget some things, especially the terrible things. My father was like that. I hope our children won't be like him and me. I still can't forget certain things, Hannah. I still can't."

And for the next few seconds, Hannah knew he was re-playing in his mind that horrible experience with the Mohawk Brave such a long time ago.

"And speaking of children," said Hannah after the somber expression left his face...

CHAPTER 16
TWINS

Samuel's face brightened after the words said by his wife broke through his momentary depression. "Hannah. Hannah. You mean... are you saying..."

"Yes, my dear Samuel, you're going to be a father. Well, at least in six or seven more months. You're a very fast worker. Marriage and soon after, a child."

"That's wonderful, Hannah. I can't believe it. I always wanted to be a father! When did it happen?"

"You should know. You've been very affectionate lately. Unusually aggressive for you, I might add. And so soon after our marriage!"

"Sorry. Sometimes you make me so happy that...is it going to be a girl or boy?"

"How could I know, my sweet husband. We'll know when the time comes. Unless you want to ask one of those Indian medicine men to find out!"

"Of course not, Hannah. That's the last thing I'd want to do. I better start checking with one of the three doctors on the island - or perhaps, you might want Mrs. Adams, the midwife?"

"We'll see, Samuel. We have time. But, if we can't get Dr.

Marshall in Smithtown, which is far from here, we'll use Mrs. Adams. She has a very good reputation. We'll see."

"OK. Do you think we should at least start planning what name we should give the baby?"

"No harm in that. Although, as I said, we still have a lot of time."

"We'd have to think of a name if it's a girl or if it's a boy."

"Or three names if we have triplets, Samuel. Since I became with child soon after our marriage, anything's, possible!"

"Quit teasing me, Hannah. I would still be happy, but getting triplets, or even twins, is not only a very, very big responsibility, but it's also a remote possibility!"

"It could happen, Samuel. It happened to Mrs. Hendricks, and she was thirty-two years old...triplets...amazing."

"Knowing you, Hannah, you probably have a list of names already made up."

"As a matter of fact, I do. Want to hear them? If it is a girl, how about Martha, my mother's name. Especially since it would please my father and mother who are very sickly. I hope they live to see our first child."

"I'm sure they will. I like the name, Martha. Agreed."

"How about the name Samuel, if it's a boy? I'd have two Samuels in the family!"

"That's nice and very thoughtful, but I think you have enough to contend with just one me."

"Then how about your father's name...Nathaniel? It sounds like a good English, colonial name."

"That would be nice. I like the name, and it will keep reminding me of my father."

"Fine. It's all settled then, Samuel."

"What if we really have triplets," said Samuel in jest.

"Then I'll hit you over the head with a broomstick and tell you to keep your trousers on!"

"Oh, Hannah, sometimes you can be so bawdy," said Samuel, who then hugged and kissed his wife.

Ironically, they had to use both names. The twins, Martha and Nathaniel, were born in late December, 1748, as a beaming Samuel and exhausted Mrs. Adams looked on.

CHAPTER 17
EIGHT YEARS

For eight years, until 1758, they couldn't have been happier, watching their children grow and their business continue to prosper as even more settlers moved into the territory. Their children from an early age were taught the virtues of tolerance, moral rectitude, and the importance of family unity.

The only discordant note was the growing desire of Hiram, like Jabez Brown, to return to his native England. His elderly parents and two sisters were still living in a country village ten miles north of London. Hiram also missed the excitement of historic London with its plethora of plays, minstrel shows, pubs, and street entertainers. The absence in London of wild animals and Indians and their strange customs also contributed to his decision.

"You know," he told Samuel, "I'm starting to miss England. London, my old friends, and what's left of my family. I've been thinking of selling you my half of the business and returning to England." Surprised at his sudden decision, Samuel tried briefly to discourage Hiram from leaving, but his efforts were unsuccessful.

"I'm told, Samuel, that New Amsterdam, now called New York, in 1664 was similar somewhat to what London looked like – at least some of it - when I left for, what some people are now calling,

'America.' Even if I lived here in the 1660's, I would have felt even less comfortable in the midst of all these Indians and wild animals roaming through the woods. I have to admit, like Hannah, I'm not comfortable being around these sav...Indians. They seem harmless and respectful, but sometimes I have the uneasy feeling that they, all of a sudden, could explode with anger and violence."

"Maybe," said Samuel, "one or two here and there would get drunk or violent, but that's the exception - the same holds true with some of the white settlers. Most of the Algonquin Indians are a peaceful, humble lot devoted to hunting, planting, fishing, and family."

"And sometimes fighting each other, Samuel."

"True, but that's also rare, especially around here. So many Algonquins now are not only customers but also my friends."

Resigned to losing his valued friend and partner, he reluctantly settled accounts with Hiram who sold his half of the store to Samuel for a very reasonable price. Hiram then booked passage on the next schooner leaving from New York Harbor to Portsmouth, England.

As a courtesy to their friend, Hannah and Samuel accompanied Hiram as they went by horse and wagon and then by ferry across the East River. For a small fee, the horse and wagon until their return were taken care of by a young man. Hiram was content to travel with little luggage but with a substantial amount of money, mostly English currency. The trip wouldn't take very long since the hired dugout canoe was boarded at the narrowest point on the East River, 200 yards, from Manhattan.

They didn't notice Samuel shiver as he helped put several pieces of luggage into the canoe. If they did, they probably would have attributed it to a cold wind moving in from the west and ruffling the river water. Samuel's mind had uncontrollably flashed back to the time, after Huggins was killed, when he stepped into a similar canoe and headed for the Dutch trading post up river. Despite his trembling, Samuel still wished the river trip were longer since he would have had more time to talk to Hiram whom he and Hannah would never see again.

Later, they watched as Hiram boarded the American schooner Sultan, a three-mast fore-and-aft rigged ship. On ship, Hiram waved good-bye as did the ship's other passengers to those seeing them depart.

The ship's passenger agent had told Hiram that the Sultan could move as easily in the deep water of the Atlantic Ocean as it could in shallow-water ports. The ship at sea would travel between 20 to 30 leagues daily, the time depending on wind currents, as it made the approximately eight-week trip across the Atlantic Ocean.

"I heard that there are pirate ships along the coast," Hiram had said to the agent. "Are they a problem?"

"No sir. We have ten seamen on board. And they are experts in handling the schooner's six guns. And this ship has three, and not two, masts. They'll get us to England faster. Don't worry about pirates, sir. This is 1758. We've had this type of reliable and safe schooner for almost one hundred years. And, if need be, like the naval frigate, it can outrun any pirate ship!" This information told also to Samuel diminished the fears he had for his good friend's ocean passage.

"We'll miss him terribly," said Hannah, with her voice choking. "Too bad the children are in Sunday School. I know, they'll miss their Uncle Hiram!"

After they had picked up the children at the newly established Anglican Church, Samuel tied their horse and wagon to the horizontal wood railing at their cottage. Samuel, for some reason, then thought about the early Indians, such as those in the 1500's and 1600's, who travelled mostly by foot or by canoe on the island's many streams and rivers. Now, horses introduced from Europe enabled the Indians, as well as settlers, to travel further and faster. This must be beneficent progress, thought Samuel. He seemed to feel, however, that he was somehow in the midst of unstoppable and unpredictable radical change. The cold wind was rushing more swiftly as they entered their home.

CHAPTER 18

IROQUOIS ATTACK

After Hiram had left, despite Samuel's last minute pleas, Hannah had worked even longer to help her husband. She told Samuel that even if he hired a full-time assistant she would still work in the store at least three or four days a week. Samuel had stammered and objected, but he was secretly happy to be with his wife more often and to admire how sweetly and diplomatically she treated all of the customers. In fact, many asked for her specifically when they first came into the store.

Hannah had complimented her husband on his knowledge of Indian ways, but he thought it unimportant to tell her in detail about "tributes" which the more powerful subtribes still exacted over weaker ones. These tribute-demanding subtribes in the middle 1700's included the Iroquois, who dominated the weaker Canarsies and even the Narrangansetts in Connecticut and occasionally the less influential but still strong Montauks.

The Canarsies, unknown to Samuel, had been quietly paying the tribute (usually consisting of wampum, deer and bear skins, and dried clams) at least once a year to the Iroquois located in and north of the town of New York. Unlike the old cruel Pequots and present day Narragansetts, the Iroquois usually did not abduct squaws. If they did, they would seize young Indian squaws to replace those who died or who were stolen by other Indians.

Some of the remaining important Dutch officials in New York had tried to persuade the Canarsies to pay them the tribute instead of to the Iroquois in return for Dutch protection. But the Dutch reneged on their promise because of diminished political and military power to do so and a genuine lack of concern for "those unimportant heathens across the East River." Expecting to be protected by the Dutch authorities, the Canarsies in 1758 paid no tribute. Samuel, however, did tell his wife that lately he had been hearing some disturbing stories about friction between the Canarsies and the Iroquois.

"Have you heard anything, Hannah, about some squabbling between our Indian friends here and the Iroquois?"

"It's odd that you said that because several customers have mentioned that there apparently has been recent communication between the Canarsies Chief and the Dutch or English officials across the river. About what, I don't know." If Hannah had known the answer, she would have insisted that her family immediately travel eastward until it would be safe to return.

On that last Thursday in December, 1758, in the early morning, 150 Iroquois, intending to massacre and plunder the Canarsies, quietly crossed the East River in 15 large dugout canoes, each carrying 10 warriors, and had assembled at the shore a mile northeast of Canarsies Town. A few very young warriors, despite their objections, were assigned to guard the long dugouts.

Samuel was in the back storage room of the Tyler General Store (for sentimental reasons he kept the original name). In the front sales part of the store, his wife was sweeping the wood floor as their children, each eight years old, played a traditional Algonquin's game of spinning tops. The toys were made of small, shaped pieces of wood. Martha preferred playing with her dolls, but to please her brother,

Nathaniel, she would always defer to his preferences.

Samuel would smile with pleasure as he heard his children laugh at each other's attempt to prolong the spinning of the tops. As he was standing on a ladder and reaching for a box on the top shelf, there was a sudden silence. Then he heard such a terrifying scream that he almost fell backward before regaining his balance. Alarmed and frightened, he scrambled down the remaining steps of the ladder and hurried to open the door leading to the front of the store. Samuel froze in horror and disbelief as he saw the motionless Hannah lying on the floor with blood streaming from the wound in her head.

"Oh, my God, oh my God! Hannah! Hannah!" He knelt next to her and cradled her in his arms, crying at what his eyes saw but which his mind could not and did not want to comprehend.

Unaware of nothing around him except his wife, he did not see another and different Iroquois Brave push open the front door and release an arrow which pierced Samuel's chest. For whatever reason, unlike the other Brave who used a tomahawk to kill Hannah, he preferred the bow and arrow. In close quarters, the Iroquois usually killed not with a bow and arrow but with a knife or a club with an axe at its tip.

There were then no children there - only the silence of death and the ghoulish spectre of a dead husband - whose luck had run out - still embracing his lifeless wife.

CHAPTER 19
BROKEN FAMILY

As he ran out of the store in shock and confusion, young Nathaniel later realized he should have stayed to protect his sister, wherever she was, and look for his father somewhere in the rear of the store. But the horrifying sight of that garishly painted Indian warrior glaring at his dead mother, and then at him, made the eight-year old so fearful that his instinct was to run as fast as he could past the Iroquois Brave.

After running almost fifty yards, he stopped, breathless, with sweat running down his face, and fear causing his hands to shake. Despite what must have been tremendous trauma for an eight-year old, he felt that he had to go back to his parents and do what he could, if anything, to help his father and look for his sister.

After he rounded the side of his father's store, his face turned white at the sight of a large Indian blocking him and mounted on the largest white horse he had ever seen. His simple headdress consisted of white feathers, mixed with red and yellow ones, matching the dyes on his face and bare upper chest. Next to his leggings and attached to the saddle were the weapons of war: a tomahawk, long knife, and a smaller dagger. Unlike the six Braves behind him, he had no bows and arrows carried in a sling across his shoulder.

Nathaniel, like any eight-year old, was very frightened, under the circumstances, at the sight of these battle-ready Indians in the midst of a tribute war between the Iroquois and the Canarsies and the latter's supporters, the Massapequas.

Nathaniel stared with fear at the great Chief Tackapousha of the Massapequas, but he became calm when he saw that a kindly and friendly face was looking down at him. Nathaniel's body relaxed, and suddenly he didn't feel threatened because of the comforting appearance of this man who somehow reminded him of his father.

"And who are you, my young friend?" asked the Chief in softly spoken English words.

Nathaniel was surprised at hearing the large Indian speak in such clear and precise English.

'Don't be afraid, child. We won't harm you. Tell us who you are."

"I am Nathaniel Townsend. My father owns the General Store over there."

The chief looked in that direction, and a worried look crossed his face.

"How old are you, young Nathaniel?"

"I am eight years old, sir. And how old are you?"

The Chief laughed and so did his warriors until he looked back at them.

"I am Chief Tackapousha, Nathaniel. Let us find your father." With one sweep of his hand, he deposited Nathaniel behind him on the horse.

"My mother and sister are also in there, sir."

"We'll find them."

When the Chief stopped near the front door, he motioned two Braves to look inside. After several minutes, they came out with sorrowful expressions on their faces. In rapidly spoken Algonquin words, so that Nathaniel hopefully would not understand, they said that the man and woman were dead - the woman by a tomahawk and the man with an Iroquois arrow. They said there was no one else in the store.

"No little girl?" asked Chief Tackapousha in Algonquin.

"No. No one else, Chief. No girl."

It was obvious to the Chief that Nathaniel's sister probably must have been kidnapped by the Iroquois and brought to their camp across the East and Hudson Rivers. Chief Tackapousha turned around and was about to say something until he saw tears roll down Nathaniel's face. Perhaps the boy surmised what might have happened. The Chief, visibly moved, said nothing but wondered if Nathaniel had suspected the worst about both parents and his sister.

The Canarsies subtribe would have been completely overwhelmed and massacred by the Iroquois if they hadn't asked for and received help from the Massapequas. The Chiefs of the Canarsies and Massapequas were honorary blood brothers and felt obligated to help each other.

The war would not have occurred if the Dutch leaders in New York had not falsely promised to defend the Canarsies if they paid tribute to the Dutch and not to the Iroquois. The Dutch political leaders reneged on their promise which led to the Iroquois to more boldly seek revenge by attacking the Canarsies. Thanks to an Indian informant in New York, the Canarsies had enough time to enlist the aid of the Massapequas who arrived just in time to successfully help thwart to a large extent the Iroquois sneak War Party attack.

On the ride back to the Massapequas' camp, Nathaniel prayed that somehow his father and sister were alive, and if not, as he was taught in religious Sunday school, that they would safely be in Heaven.

Chief Tackapousha could hear the boy's occasional sobbing and hear his low murmuring of religious prayers as Nathaniel held onto Chief Tackapousha as if there were no other security in the world.

CHAPTER 20
SECOND HOME

In the journey to Chief Tackapousha's settlement, Nathaniel alternated between thinking of his family and dozing. He vaguely remembered the Chief offering him a cup of water that one of his Braves had scooped from a slow moving stream.

Nathaniel was unaware of some white settlers who had watched intently as the almost 200 warriors moved silently down a main woodland trail. He didn't notice the scampering of various frightened animals, such as bears, deer, and turkeys retreating deeper into the darkness of the woods. When he was not sleeping, his mind kept reviewing what had happened in the store before he ran away.

As they neared the camp, Chief Tackapousha asked, "Are you all right, young Nathaniel?"

Nathaniel could only say, "I think so, sir."

Outside his large Wigwam, the Chief dismounted and then lifted Nathaniel down from his horse. He carried the half-asleep Nathaniel and gently put him on a sleeping mat inside the Wigwam. As Nathaniel lapsed deeply back into sleep, he again felt comforted by the gentleness and compassion of the man who was treating him so kindly.

Outside the dwelling, Chief Tackapousha told one of his Braves to "find Arandel and tell her I want her to keep this boy company and to comfort him. She will be good for him. They are both about the same age."

The Chief would have sent his wife, if she had not died last winter of pneumonia. But, the Chief had so much faith that his precocious eight-year old daughter, despite her young age, would be able to comfort Nathaniel that he didn't regret his decision.

Nathaniel woke up and realized where he was only after a brief but intense examination of the Wigwam's interior. The flaps, tied to each side of the only entrance, would be released, he thought, only when the unseasonably mild weather ended.

The area was fifteen feet in diameter with the ground hollowed out to almost three feet deep. In the middle was a large clay pot simmering with meat and vegetables above a fire almost extinguished. He looked into the pot and was so hungry that he was tempted to scoop something out of it if he could locate the proper utensil. He guessed that inside the pot were venison or bear meat and possibly a mixture of vegetables, including what looked like corn, squash, and tomatoes. Glancing upward, he noted that the opening at the top of the Wigwam enabled the smoke from the fire to escape.

Nathaniel also realized that he had been sleeping on a four-foot wide woven mat on a bench which circled the inside of the dwelling. Above the wood benches and supported by poles were shelves filled with food such as smoked bear and deer meat, dried clams, and assorted smoked fish. In bowls made of wood and pottery were fish, fruits, berries, and vegetables. The pottery, he later learned, was made by Indian Squaws from moist clay hardened by heat. In one corner was an array of bows and arrows, knives, and tomahawks, all of which frightened Nathaniel.

As he wondered what was going to happen to him, he heard light footsteps approaching the entrance. Alarmed, he didn't know what to do: hide, which was impossible, run past whoever was entering, grab one of the weapons which he did not know how to use, or do what apparently was the only thing he could - wait and see who entered.

As he began trembling, he saw a young Indian squaw, about his age, enter the Wigwam and smile at him. The smile, so broad, so kind, had to be that of a friendly person, he thought.

She took a few steps toward him, but stopped when she saw Nathaniel stiffen and move back slightly on the bench. He saw a red and yellow ribbon circling her forehead and her medium-length straight black hair just touching her shoulders. On her very light brown skin, she had simple red, white, and yellow designs on her face and body. He was amazed that she had such clear blue eyes which fascinated him. Nathaniel thought she was very beautiful.

"My name is Arandel, and what is your name, little boy?" She knew what it was because her father's messenger had told her, but she wanted to hear it from him.

"I'm not little, and I'm not a little boy!" said Nathaniel suddenly gathering courage.

Well, you're not a big man yet, and you're not a girl, or are you? What are you then, and who are you?"

I'm Nathaniel…Nathaniel Townsend, and I'm not a sissy girl. I'm a big boy."

She smiled so nicely and so sweetly that any fear or uncertainty that he might have had toward her, melted away.

Then, looking at her less fearfully and more calmly, he realized that she was bare-chested, and she smiled again as she saw his face redden.

"You're, you're…you're…"

"You're a funny little boy, Nathaniel Townsend," she said gently.

"You're very nice. I like you."

And before Nathaniel could even decide how to respond, he said, "I like you, too."

CHAPTER 21

ARANDEL

The unusual introduction began a ten-year friendship between the Indian Princess Arandel and Nathaniel who was unofficially adopted by her father since he apparently had no living relatives. They became inseparable friends as Arandel taught him the ways of the Indians, including learning the Algonquin language. At first, they seemed to be like brother and sister, with Nathaniel occasionally calling her "Martha." Arandel always forgave him his lapses because she realized that he loved his sister who was always in his memory.

Chief Tackapousha was very happy with the growing relationship between his daughter and Nathaniel. From a timid, shy boy, he had become much more confident and outgoing under her influence. The Chief, who remembered this young boy clinging to him so desperately, was pleased to see Nathaniel changing gradually into a young man.

The Chief knew that Arandel was very unusual and not because she was his only offspring. He recognized her extreme intelligence and compassion when she was just a young child playing with other Indian children. Sometimes later, when she was a pre-teenager, he caught himself talking to her as if she were one of his trusted council advisors. After his wife died, the Chief drew his only comfort in his love for his then seven-year old daughter.

Arandel did whatever she could do to please Nathaniel. Since he didn't like her face and body streaked with bright dyes, even if they were the symbolic red and yellow colors of the Massapequas, she washed them off permanently. Her father did not object to her parting with some Algonquin customs because he approved of her trying not only to please Nathaniel but also to help him adjust to a completely new culture.

Except for something randomly occurring that would remind him of his sister and mother, like the fragrance of lilacs which they both loved, he tried, but not always successfully, to forget that awful day when the Iroquois attacked his village. Much to Nathaniel's pleasure, she frequently would find for him the pink-purplish lilac flowers and arrange them carefully in a large pottery jar which she would put in his Wigwam.

What charmed Nathaniel, besides her beauty, were her pleasant voice, her always ebullient and kind personality, and mischievous but playful sense of humor. She would tease him as he tried to pronounce Algonquin words or as he confused the names of the many wild flowers which she had identified and described so many times. She seemed also to be in love with the natural woodland beauty of the trees and flowers and said to him so often that he could say it before she did: "The flowers and trees create the perfume of the forest."

In her early teen years, Arandel noticed that Nathaniel, especially in the summer months, was continually staring at her bare breasts - and sometimes even in the cold weather when they were concealed under a deerskin top.

"What are you looking at, young boy," she would say, and he would blush. "You look like me, Nathaniel, when your face gets red. Do you want to feel them since you like them so much?"

Nathaniel's face would get redder, and then he would mumble a few unintelligible words and silently promise himself that someday he boldly would fondle them.

When he periodically dressed like an Algonquin for a festival or just to please Arandel, she would in some dances see his bare chest, a belt holding a breechcloth around his waist, and his soft deerskin moccasins, and say, "What do you have there under your waist, Nathaniel? Show me. Let me see if you've grown up yet!" And then she would smile and laugh playfully and pretend to raise the cloth flaps and expose his nakedness underneath.

"One day," Nathaniel promised himself, "One day I'll do it! I'll surprise her. Just wait!"

A ceremony ("powwow"), usually held every few months, was intended, via magical rituals, to cure disease and promote success in battle. To please Arandel, Nathaniel would reluctantly, and somewhat awkwardly, participate in the ceremonial dancing and mystical rites. Some ceremonies required Nathaniel to wear feathers in his hair and also multi – colored clothing with special decorations – all of which made Nathaniel self – conscious and uncomfortable.

CHAPTER 22
LEARNING INDIAN WAYS

In the following years, Nathaniel could easily have been considered a Long Island Indian. Arandel taught him about the Algonquins' dependence on hunting, fishing, and planting in order to survive. She even had the Braves teach him how to make canoes and, with some regret and trepidation on Nathaniel's part, how to use the Algonquin weapons such as the bow and arrow, tomahawk, spear, and long and short knives.

Most of the cooking and planting was done by squaws, so she was able to show him how to prepare the varied meals and how correctly to bury seeds in the ground as well as cultivate the many plants such as beans, the staple corn, melon, pumpkin, squash, tobacco (a crop he had never seen before and which therefore intrigued him), tomatoes, wheat, and many more. He and Arandel spent many delightful hours picking the fruit - mainly apples, cherries, peaches, and pears. Since food should not be wasted, they playfully threw only a few at each other.

Even though he liked being with Arandel, Nathaniel thought it was still a tedious and tiresome chore plucking the many berries such as blackberries, blueberries, the scarce gooseberries, and strawberries from the wildly growing bushes in the woods near the camp. As the

Massapequas saw Nathaniel doing these tasks, they would chuckle and call Nathaniel "Arandel's little slave."

When he would get bored with his chores, she would bring him to one of the many nearby streams. He knew that the tribes always tried to settle near waterways in order to easily obtain water for drinking and cooking as well as be able to travel more easily by canoe throughout the island.

Many times Arandel would bring food and water for a mini-picnic. Nathaniel would row as far as he could down one stream or river and then stop for lunch on shore at the edge of the water. Nathaniel loved to listen to her as he paddled and she named and described the flowers and trees visible from the canoe. Nathaniel later, in looking back, realized how he treasured these little trips when Arandel seemed to mesmerize him as she looked into his eyes and described the bewitching natural wonders and the magic of a land she considered mystical and sacred.

On other occasions, she would watch as he helped Braves, positioned in deep streams and rivers, chase fish through constructed channels and then into large nets where they were trapped and easily rounded up. Some large streams, however, were filled with so many fish that they could be scooped up easily with one's hands or with a large bowl. The Massapequas also taught Nathaniel to spear fish or, in a test of skill and accuracy, to catch fish using a bow and arrow.

Fishing was also done along the shores of the Sound and the Atlantic Ocean. Arundel would always compliment him as he rounded up clams, eels, lobsters, and mussels, as well as the very large sea sturgeon, and fresh water trout. Nathaniel was amazed to learn from Arundel that lobsters caught in the waters off Manhattan could be as long as six feet. After many initial clumsy efforts, Nathaniel had become quite skilled in mastering the art of fishing.

Nathaniel particularly liked hunting which was one of the few things he remembered doing with his father. As he occasionally had accompanied his father in hunting deer and bear, his father, sometimes reluctantly but at Nathaniel's urging, would recount his experience hunting animals for furs in the Upper Hudson Valley region. But, even though his father taught him to hunt, Samuel always refrained from hunting and killing animals. Nathaniel had never realized until later how difficult it must have been for his father not only to go hunting to please him but also to reveal this painful part of his past.

Under Arandel's always watchful eye, the Massapequas would train him in the essentials of hunting: using the right weapon, setting traps, and knowing the habitats of various animals. They also told him how to determine what trails the animals usually followed and where they drank water.

What was very important in farming and hunting was the planting of corn, which was used for a variety of meals, and the killing of deer which provided not only food but also tools and weapons which were made from the antlers and other deer bones.

Nathaniel, nor the Braves, ever minded Arandel tagging along in his learning process. The Braves saw that they enjoyed each other, and whenever he did something worthy of praise, he would look in her direction and revel not only in her presence but in her looks of approval.

Even though Arandel always seemed happy and constantly praised Nathaniel for whatever he did, there was an underlying sadness which she always kept hidden - a dread of the day when he would probably leave her and re-enter the world of the white man.

CHAPTER 23
LOVE

Close to his eighteenth birthday, Arandel planned a picnic when she hoped to summon the courage to express verbally her love for him. She believed that he loved her, but that he was either too shy or afraid to tell her so. Ever since he first met her, he had trouble revealing his deepest feelings as if he were fearful of getting disappointed - or hurt - or unable to subdue the emotions of the past that would return as they sometimes did when he thought about his parents and sister.

For weeks she had planned the lunch at her special hideaway, her personal refuge that she went to when she felt anxious or sad, especially when she despaired about the possibility of Nathaniel leaving her - and worse still, falling in love with someone else. Not even her father or Nathaniel knew of this nearby hidden retreat, a little grassy area surrounded by small lilac bushes and tall pine trees.

They were so close that he wanted to be with or near her every day, but he never realized where she went when she would sometimes disappear and return an hour or so later, happy and refreshed. Nathaniel never questioned what he thought was probably her desire for privacy or other personal needs. Arandel's positive nature and faith that the Great Spirit would always help and protect her, enabled her to maintain her optimism that she would be a part of Nathaniel's future.

On that mild, warm day in August, 1768, Nathaniel watched her intently, as he always did, carefully place the rice cakes, assorted fruits and berries, and still warm tea in a ceramic pot on the thin bearskin blanket.

He never tired of looking at her and noticing how she had gradually changed physically in the past ten years. The only things that hadn't changed were her smooth light brown skin, bright blue eyes, and short straight black hair. She was now five feet, eight inches tall, with a body that had blossomed in front of his eyes, especially in the last four years. Her breasts were full and firm, and in their nakedness shook slightly with every motion. Her small waist, which she permitted Nathaniel to occasionally encircle with his eager hands, led to slender and well-exercised legs. She was very beautiful, but Nathaniel had always thought so since the time he first saw eight - year old Arandel at the entrance to her father's Wigwam - which seemed so long ago. To him, there was no other woman so wonderful – so beautiful.

For a long time, Nathaniel had resisted yielding to his sexual urges out of respect for the virginal Arandel and for her father who treated him as if he were his own son. But, in the past year, it was increasingly difficult for him and Arandel to continue to resist the strong emotional and sexual attraction they had for each other.

"I'm glad you made corn cakes. I haven't had them for a while. I always liked the way you made them. And the tea. If I remember right, you make it from flowers and goldenrod leaves mixed in boiled water. Right?"

She sat down next to him, and she was so close, that he was tempted to jump on top of her and fondle her naked breasts pointing so stiffly and invitingly at him. She was about to say something, but instead she only smiled.

"Yes, that's how I make tea, and I love to cook for you,

Nathaniel. You're so easy to please, and you're so appreciative. My father's the same way… I see you're staring at my breasts again, you naughty boy. If you like them so much, why don't you do something about it?" This was the first time he felt that she had so sincerely and convincingly invited him to do so.

He stared at her… "You mean…"

"Yes. You say you are so brave and could be one of my father's warriors. I think I'll call you my 'Golden Warrior' because of your blond hair, and if you're brave enough…"

Before she could finish, he said, "I'm not a warrior yet, but maybe someday…" Then, he moved on top of her, and since she didn't resist, he fondled her breasts and then repeatedly kissed her face and mouth.

"Oh, Nathaniel, oh, please don't stop. Please don't stop." She kissed him passionately and drew his body even more tightly against her.

He gently but impatiently untied her rope belt and then removed her short skirt. With his head resting against her breasts, he felt her spreading her legs as he carefully penetrated her. All of the pent-up longing and sexual frustration had suddenly exploded. For a long time, the only sounds in the glade were her moaning and his repeating of her name. Her climactic scream of joy could only be heard possibly by noisy blue jays in the nearby trees, an eagle soaring high overhead, and the distant sound of water in a stream surging toward a waterfall…

Arandel had pulled him down for the second time, and for a few more moments they again united in a frenzy of mutual ecstasy. Both exhausted, they got up and embraced and held each other without speaking for several minutes.

"I'm glad, I'm glad. I wanted to do that for a long time. I love you, Arandel. I've always loved you. Ever since…"

"I know, Nathaniel. I know. I love you too. You made me so happy. I'm so happy, I'm shaking!"

As they walked back to the Massapequas' settlement, holding hands, Nathaniel vowed to ask her father's permission to marry Arandel, as was the traditional Indian custom. But, no matter what her father's decision was, or if she would become pregnant or not, he was determined to marry her.

For both of them, it was the culmination of a ten-year attraction beginning when a very young Indian girl entered her father's Wigwam to console a grieving little boy who had just lost his father, mother, and probably his sister.

CHAPTER 24

APPROACHING STORM

Nathaniel and Arandel were going to approach her father about their new relationship, which they were both eager to do, until Arandel said that they should wait for a few days to tell him.

"Nathaniel, my father is going to help the Canarsies because the Iroquois are planning to attack them again. My father said the Iroquois across the river have a new Chief who wants the surrounding tribes to pay tribute as they used to."

A chill went through Nathaniel as he remembered the last time in 1758 when the Iroquois attacked Canarsies Town but fortunately were rebuffed by her father and his warriors.

"I thought tributes were a thing of the past, Arandel, because the subtribes have gotten stronger and now have the support of the white settlers and British soldiers who seem on the island to be everywhere - especially on the north shore and way out east."

"True, Nathaniel. But the Iroquois are a very stubborn and proud tribe who have always had the support of the British who appreciated their help during the French and Indian War. That's what my father told me. This new Chief wants to avenge their defeat ten years ago when…" Arandel stopped when she saw Nathaniel looking upset and troubled. She paused and waited for Nathaniel to regain his composure.

"There's no one who wants to help the Canarsies except my father. Not even the British troops in Manhattan, or the Dutch who are now too weak. In fact, most of the British soldiers are in the place that's called Boston. There is much trouble now, as you know, between the British and the settlers." Arandel couldn't have known that the friction would become so bad that in 1773, the American Revolution would result.

"I'd like to go with your father," volunteered Nathaniel. "He's done so much for me. I want to help him. After all, you said I could be a warrior."

Alarmed, Arandel quickly said, "No, Nathaniel, my father wants you to stay here to protect us, just in case."

"Protect you and the squaws and possibly a few old Braves against what, Arrie? I can do more to help in the fight against the Iroquois. You've seen how I've learned so much."

Arandel, admiring his bravery and loyalty to her father, repeated what her father had told her. "My father said there could be a problem. The Chief of the Unkechaugs, up north, said that the rumor was that Narragansetts across the bay are planning to attack tribes on the island. They had a hard winter and are looking for tributes. They might come as far south as our village although my father doubts it. They're a very violent tribe. Just in case, my father wants you and some of the old Braves and young ones to protect the women here. He wants you to stay here and take charge of protecting us!"

"Did you tell him that, Arrie?"

"No, Nathaniel. Of course not. I would never do that. I would not interfere with what you or my father wants to do. Like you, he decides for himself. He'll talk to you about it later. Although, my dear Nathaniel, I truly would like to keep you here."

"I really would like to help your father. At least I could show my appreciation and prove that I am worthy to be a warrior."

"You don't have to prove anything to me or my father, Nathaniel. If he wants you to stay behind and protect us, if necessary, he has a lot of faith in you and your courage. I know I do. You'll always be my 'Golden Warrior,' my future mate. This a time when you must be patient and wait. Your time to fight may yet come although I hope not. Pressing his head against her bosom, she kissed and embraced him."

That night, Chief Tackapousha led one hundred Braves eastward toward the Canarsies territory. The loud rumbling sound of the horses not only disturbed the silence of the night but sent the wild animals - small and large - scurrying for safety.

As he neared Canarsies Town in the early morning, Chief Tackapousha recalled the sad time when he had first met Nathaniel. The little boy, now almost fully grown at eighteen, had clung to him then as if he were Nathaniel's father. He smiled as he thought of Arandel and Nathaniel growing up together with his daughter acting as surrogate mother and friend. He was happy at how their relationship had flourished and was certain that they truly loved each other.

Approaching Canarsies Town where he would soon engage the invading Iroquois, he contemplated how the natural beauty of the surrounding area conflicted with the ugly conflict that was about to happen. He had led his warriors through a small swamp and then a patch of woods filled with many trees and a host of wild flowers. He remembered, for some reason, teaching Arandel the names of all the trees - such as the chestnut, maple, oak, and pine - and the flowers which she loved to pick and present to him and her mother. And she did all this at such a young age! The Chief also thought about his confidence in Nathaniel to protect the remaining tribe members against a possible but unlikely attack by the Narragansetts of Connecticut.

As far back as 1672 when King Charles of England granted a charter to establish Connecticut, which included dominion over what was then called Paumanok, and not Long Island, the cruel Pequots and then the Narragansetts considered it their implied right to plunder the island tribes to demand tribute. Paumanok ("land of tribute") was, thus, a fitting name for a land where the weaker Algonquins were continually forced to pay tribute in the 1600's and early 1700's.

A few hours later, one hundred Narragansetts had bypassed subtribes in the middle north part of the island, and had decided to attack the Massapequas and then the Merricks in anticipation of much greater tribute such as wampum, food, and also the abduction of young squaws to replenish the diminishing numbers of their own females. The squaws would be used as sexual partners and workers for their Braves.

After crossing the Sound in long canoes, the warriors stole many horses from the weaker Unkeckhaugs and from helpless neighboring farmers. Use of the horses would enable them to move more quickly to reach and attack the unsuspecting and therefore vulnerable inhabitants of Chief Tackapousha's camp.

CHAPTER 25

SADNESS

Nathaniel and Arandel were still asleep when they were abruptly awakened by a sudden burst of loud cries and screams. Their separate wigwams, on the southern and also opposite sides of the small Indian village, were just being covered by early morning sunlight.

Arandel, at first, was uncertain as to what was happening, but Nathaniel immediately identified the screams as those of Indian squaws and the shouts as those of attacking Indians. The dim memories of the war cries of Iroquois Indians ten years ago resounded in his mind, and for a brief moment he seemed to be back in time.

Then, when he realized that he must act quickly since the village was under attack, he hurriedly put on his leggings, shirt, and moccasins and then reached for his pistol, long knife, and tomahawk. He jumped onto his horse outside the Wigwam and headed toward the tumult emanating from the northern end of the camp.

Nathaniel soon met a trio of Narrangansetts aiming their tomahawks at him as their horses were almost upon him. Swinging his tomahawk, he slashed at the three, cutting two in the chest and one on the head. In another rushing group, he killed two Braves with blows to their throats, and another with a slash across his chest. Nathaniel fought so furiously that, as the legend says, he mobilized and inspired the left behind young and old Massapequa Braves to fight with ferocious determination and courage. Those who survived said that their fellow warrior, Nathaniel, must have single-handedly killed at least forty of the enemy and injured fifteen others.

As the remaining Narragansetts retreated back toward the north and the Sound, Nathaniel's horse was bumped by a riderless horse, and as he was thrown to the ground he dropped his tomahawk. As an enemy warrior five yards away ran at him, Nathaniel threw his dagger which plunged into his chest.

According to the legend of the "Golden Warrior" that would later often be repeated, it was said that the enemy was so amazed that a blond-haired non-Indian could fight so furiously and heroically that the Great Spirit certainly must have guided his hands.

But as the legend sadly notes, at the end of the battle, as fate would have it, one of the remaining Narrangansetts was the slightly injured enemy Chief, still on his horse, who was enraged at the apparent unexpected defeat of his warriors.

Chief Winigret saw that the unaware Nathaniel was off his horse and was turning his back to him. At that moment, Arandel who had been safely observing the scene from the side of a wigwam, saw the enemy Chief, tomahawk in hand, charge at Nathaniel's back. Arandel screamed, ran toward Nathaniel, and pushed him aside just as Chief Winigret's blow smashed into her head, killing her instantly.

Nathaniel, in a state of unimaginable disbelief and horror, pulled the Chief off his horse and, instead of using his knife or tomahawk, put his hands around his throat and choked him with all the strength he possessed. Several of Chief Tackapousha's also distraught Braves eventually had to pull him away from the long dead Narragansett Chieftain. Kneeling down and sobbing, Nathaniel kept saying "Arandel, Arandel" as his fellow warriors stood silently and grieved with him...

When Chief Tackapousha returned half an hour later, he was told what had happened and with only a twitching betraying emotion on his impassive face, he walked slowly toward his Wigwam as if he were trying to delay the inevitable. Inside the Wigwam, his body froze but his emotions were crying inside him. He saw his beautiful daughter, who had been so full of life and so comforting since the death of his wife, lying on a bench mat. He couldn't speak as his throat tightened, and his hands began trembling.

Nathaniel was on the dirt floor kneeling next to her, with his body swaying back and forth and his face covered with tears. He kept moaning. "If only I hadn't turned away, if only I had turned around…It should have been me…oh, Arandel, Arandel." And he thought the world had ended for him.

Chief Tackapousha knelt, put his arm around Nathaniel, and for the first time since his wife died, he felt the rush of uncontrollable tears. In a centuries-old Algonquin chant, he prayed for the Great Spirit to take his beautiful and only child into His arms.

CHAPTER 26
AFTERMATH

There was no way for Nathaniel to be consoled. For the rest of 1768 and the first three months of 1769 he stayed by himself, barely eating, and talking to no one except occasionally to Arandel's father. Chief Tackapousha was deeply worried that Nathaniel's depression caused by his daughter's death was not lessening as the cold winter snow began disappearing in late March of 1769.

The memories of Arandel became too difficult for him to endure in the camp which held too many reminders of her presence: her greeting him with a smile, a kiss, and an embrace, her teasing and loving laugh, and so much more. What was extremely painful was to remember her when she also was eight years old, talking so sweetly to him and making him comfortable among her friends and helping the sad little boy adjust to a new life.

Many times he would walk by her wigwam and pause as if he expected her to respond to his calling her name by coming out smiling and with hands outstretched. The squaws and Braves would sorrowfully watch him as Nathaniel, near tears, would walk quickly away. Finally, Nathaniel out of necessity but with much regret, decided to leave the Indian village and live in a small cabin several miles to the north. There, perhaps, he would not constantly be haunted by the past.

One night, in his cabin, after many weeks of grieving, he wondered what Arandel would tell him to do. Her words had always been loving and encouraging and had made him feel that no one in the world was more important to her than he was.

After fitfully falling asleep, he dreamed that she had appeared and talked to him, with a smiling and concerned face, and with the usual red and yellow feathers in her hair.

"My Golden Warrior, you make me sad. I want you to remember me, but I also want you to be happy. Find someone to love the way you loved me. That would make me very happy."

He woke up with a start, looked around the room, and didn't see her, but he thought he felt her presence. Her voice and words seemed so real to him and typically always so concerned with his welfare. Still basking contently in his dream, he decided to not only find a job to support himself but also hopefully lessen the pain but never eliminate the memories of Arandel and her love.

After making some inquiries, he learned that the workers in the steadily booming whaling industry, which began as a serious business in the 1600's, were not only in demand but were also among the highest paid on the island. The whale oil, the even more valuable sperm, and whalebone were selling at very high prices in the colonies and overseas. Thus, in the summer of 1769, Nathaniel applied for a job in the whaling industry.

CHAPTER 27
A WHALER

Before becoming a more highly paid whaleboat crewman or harpooner, new workers were first assigned to the task of building or repairing whaleboats made from the wood of the plentiful cedar trees. Upon successful apprenticeship, they would be eligible to become whaler crewmen or harpooners.

The new whaleboats, some as long as fifteen feet, were patterned after the Algonquin method of constructing them with the very light but strong and durable cedar wood. Since Nathaniel had learned to help make the non - birch canoes in Chief Tackapousha's village, he quickly impressed his supervisors with his skill, knowledge, and efficiency.

The smaller canoes and larger whaleboats were sometimes bought at reasonable prices from the Indians by the whaling company, with payment in wampum, food, tobacco, and sometimes with whale fins and tails. Nathaniel's' company also hired skilled workers to build the large whaleboats, according to certain specifications, for their own business or for sale to other whaling firms. Nathaniel's job was to help construct the whaling boats, and then paint the company's name on each side.

It was more economical for the company to build whaleboats by first cutting down large cedar trees. By coincidence Nathaniel, Whaleman

Burroughs, and Shanghai Jim, plus four Indians, were assigned to a boat-making group. Unlike the Indians, the company's workers used sharp metal and not stone axes to bring down the trees. They placed moist mud or clay several feet high around the tree trunk to contain the fire. As the fire burned the bottom of the tree, the four men swung their metal axes at the burning area. Nathaniel knew that if the bark around the bottom of the tree was stripped, the tree would soon die and be easier to cut down. But his employers rejected this idea because it would be more time-consuming and therefore unprofitable.

After cutting off the branches, the tree trunk was hollowed with the metal axes. The larger trunks were used for making whaleboats, and the smaller trunks for canoes. The smaller canoes were used specifically for travelling or for fishing in the island waterways.

Nathaniel immersed himself so totally in the labor and in developing friendships, especially with Whaleman and Shanghai Jim, that his emotional pain, while not eliminated, was greatly dulled. After several months, he was, like his two friends, considering applying for a position as a more highly paid harpooner, and if not successful, as a crewman in the large whaleboats searching for, chasing, and killing whales.

Nathaniel, among the many things he had learned in Chief Tackapousha's village, was that the original whalers, since 1640, actually were the Indians. At first, the whales were either found washed ashore because of illness or storms or they were hunted close to shore. However, in the 1700's, the influx of white settlers who became whalers depleted the beached and off - shore availability of whales so extensively that it was necessary to hunt them further and further out in the Atlantic Ocean.

Whale hunting by Indians in the late 1500's and 1600's, Nathaniel was told, was then a dangerous and amateurish undertaking.

The Indian whaling bark canoes then were fragile and easily
unbalanced, especially in the sometimes unruly storm-driven waters
of the Sound, also referred to by Indians as "The Devil's Belt," and
particularly in the Atlantic Ocean. The sharpened wood but non-metal
harpoons required numerous assaults on a whale before it might
be subdued and towed, with much difficulty, back to shore. Many
Algonquins in the 1500's and 1600's lost their lives or were seriously
hurt when the small quartz-tipped wood harpoons snapped, with
the large unsubdued sea creatures usually slamming into their bark
canoes.

Nathaniel knew that only the strongest men who were also good
swimmers were selected to be whaleboat crewmen or harpooners.
He and his friends had many conversations about who would be
picked first for these lucrative jobs. Eventually, all three were selected
as crewmen and again by coincidence were assigned to the same
whaleboat.

The humorous bantering and camaraderie of the three led to
their becoming close friends on the job and during their time off. They
liked to spend most of their evenings relaxing in the few local taverns,
drinking too much beer or rum, and, except for Nathaniel, flirting with
the usually receptive white waitresses.

For different reasons, each man saved part of his salary which
usually consisted of English shillings. Whaleman was saving to build a
large tavern with rooms rented to transients, and Shanghai Jim wanted
to return to his native Shanghai. Nathaniel wanted to save enough
money perhaps to own some kind of business or travel as far as he
could into the western wilderness hopefully in order to forget...

Unfortunately for Shanghai, five years ago, hired thugs in
Shanghai carried the very drunk and "Shanghaied" Chinaman to a
schooner headed for the New World colonies. When he woke up, he

was given the choice of working as a seaman for the duration of the journey or being thrown off the ship which was several miles from port. The choice was easy to make.

One facet of his job which upset Nathaniel was the treatment by owners of their Indian workers who were shown no respect and were paid as little as possible. Usual payment for the "Savages," which some of the owners occasionally called them, was liquor and very small quantities of the killed whale, such as fins, tails, blubber, and sometimes whalebone and whale oil. They also were offered cheap clothing and occasionally powder and shot. Surprisingly, some Algonquins preferred the tail and fins of the dead whale instead of the more valuable head and blubber which contained the highly valued whale oil.

Indians, because of their agility, determination, marksmanship, and fearless attitude, were well – suited in the 1500's and 1600's to be harpooners. Because of their knowledge and skill in making smaller canoes, they also were hired in the latter part of the 1700's to help construct the larger whaleboats which had to be durable enough to withstand the rigors of whale hunting further out in the Atlantic Ocean.

As more and more whales were killed a mile or two from shore, it was necessary to go much further into the ocean to find them. Large-sized ships, carrying whaleboats, sometimes had to travel dozens of miles from shore. Eventually, in the early 1800's large sailing ships had to travel far south of the island, go around the tip of South America, and then head north. The whalers, including many off-season farmers, were sometimes away from their families during the entire whaling season which extended generally from December to late March or early April.

But in 1769, Nathaniel, Whaleman, and Shanghai Jim so impressed their supervisors that they had quickly been promoted to whaleboat crewmen. Nathaniel, because of his obvious skill displayed as an oarsman and his deft accuracy in handling and throwing the iron harpoon and lance, was soon promoted to a lead harpooner. The promotion resulted in constant ribbing by Nathaniel's two friends.

"Hey, it's not fair, Nathaniel. You had a head start learning all these things in Chief Tackapousha's camp!" complained the pretending - to - be upset Whaleman.

"I'm surprised," added Shanghai Jim, "that they didn't ask you, instead of a blacksmith, to also make the harpoon, lance, and oar rings! Since you apparently can do just about everything!"

The day before his first outing as a harpooner, a newly hired worker from the Shinnecock subtribe, looked quizzically at Nathaniel and then said, with great respect, "Are you not the famed one they call the 'Golden Warrior'? Why do you not still fight with Chief Tackapousha?"

Nathaniel, who had never been asked that question, felt the fleeting pain, and then answered, "I believe it is the will of the Great Spirit that I now do this."

The Algonquin, still looking at Nathaniel in awe, nodded, and then replied, "And so it should be."

CHAPTER 28
HARPOONER

The tall, overweight, red-haired Whaleman, so named because of his excessive girth and weight, and the diminutive Shanghai Jim, with his very short black hair on top of his decidedly unattractive face with his always twinkling eyes, were on another round of rum drinks the night before their maiden trip as whaleboaters.

"I hope tomorrow the whale doesn't bump you, Nathaniel, and then us into the Atlantic Ocean. The whales don't know they shouldn't mess with such a big hero!"

"Don't worry, Whaleman, I'll save you and bring you back to shore."

"I hope you're strong enough to swim two miles, especially if Shanghai Jim, here, also needs help!'

"Don't worry, Whaleman," said Shanghai. I may not be a great lover, but I can certainly out swim you. With all your weight, you'd probably sink, and I'd have to drag you and the whale back."

"I doubt that, Shanghai. But I'm worried about Nathaniel. Harpooning is a very dangerous business. You can get tangled up in the harpoon line, get hurt by the whale, or get thrown into the ocean, hopefully alive. I know you're strong enough, Nathaniel, but the whale is a mighty big creature that you have to hit in the right spot with your harpoon or lance. Sometimes there's no second chance. Look at what happened to Jonny Martin. The whale took a swipe at him, and he never had a chance. Died on the spot!"

"Killing the whale with the right harpoon blow to the head," warned Shanghai, is not the only thing we have to worry about, Whaleman."

"You mean dragging the whale back to shore, Shanghai?"

"Yes. Even if Nathaniel kills that monster, we still have to put tie lines into it and bring it to shore. That's why the crewmen are selected - because of their muscles."

"Now, Shanghai, you're telling me you have muscles. They look more like pimples to me!"

"Look, Whaleman, I proved I could handle the job. They said so in our training."

"Yeah, you're right, Shanghai. For a little guy, you've got a few muscles - and not just the ones between your legs!"

"Don't be a wise guy, my big friend. We'll see what's what tomorrow."

"I hope so. Tomorrow we'll start earning real money and so will those savages in our boat."

"They're not savages, Whaleman" said Nathaniel. "I don't know how you can say that. Just because they're a different color or they're not paid what they should be? Most of them, in my experience, except the early 1600's savage Pegquots, and the Narragansetts in Connecticut and perhaps some Mohawks near Canada, are very friendly, peaceful, and hardworking."

"I'm sorry, Nathaniel. I spoke too quickly and foolishly. I know you lived among the Algonquins for ten years, and you know them better than I do. Sorry, my young friend."

Nathaniel accepted Whaleman's apology, and was again

impressed with the big man's sincerity and understanding of Nathaniel's sensitivity about how the Algonquins were regarded.

Shanghai tried to change the subject. "Did I tell you how I was Shanghaied…"

"About a hundred times," interrupted Whaleman. And a thousand times how the women here ignore you or, if they're prostitutes, charge you triple!"

"Well, they're always laughing at me. They call me the ugly Chinaman, especially the English ladies. What do you call them… lassies…with the big…"

"Oh, they do it because they're having fun with you," said Whaleman, "You get so nervous. I heard one of them say that," Whaleman, trying half-heartedly to make Shanghai feel better, added "That's just because you have a little…" Both Whaleman and Nathaniel started laughing.

"You fellows are supposed to be my friends. Instead you're making fun of me."

"Oh, come on, Shanghai, we're just joking. Let's talk about something else."

"Ok, Whaleman, tell us how you've become such an expert on whales. It might put us to sleep!"

"Well, I'll tell you, small one," said Whaleman as he picked up his rum mug. "Tomorrow we help bring many things to society."

"Stuff it, Whaleman. I was just kidding. No more of your pompous lectures!"

"As I was saying," continued Whaleman, ignoring Shanghai's interruption, "we get a lot of things from the sperm whale. Besides oil for lamps, there's whalebone, blubber, and from the whales' head, they can produce soap, beauty products, cooking oil, and ambergris which is turned into what they call perfume."

"Are you kidding, Whaleman!" blurted Shanghai. I wouldn't eat or use anything from that smelly whale, especially the blubber!"

"So much for your knowledge of whale products and cooking, Shanghai," admonished Whaleman who was beginning to slur his words. If you don't like whale meat, which I don't, you can feed it to the cows, horses, sheep…or your girlfriend if you can find one!"

"Better to feed the animals than me. And if I wanted, I could get a girlfriend…"

"Maybe an old squaw," said Whaleman, almost spilling his drink.

"Very humorous, Whaleman, very humorous."

"Now, back to… to whaling. According to this little article I read that was printed in the N.Y Gazette, the whalebone from the whale's mouth can be made into ladies' corsets and parasols."

"Never heard of them. What are they?"

"I'll explain it to you later, Shanghai," said Nathaniel. "You apparently are not familiar with ladies' things!" Both of Shanghai's friends smiled.

"And, my little Chinese friend, did you know that there are four major types of whales around here, all slow moving?"

"I don't know, Whaleman. I never asked them," responded Shanghai, laughing at what he considered a clever retort.

"You might have a chance tomorrow, little Jim. Anyway, there's the gray humpback, which are usually found near the coast, the sperm, the bowhead, and the gray. I bet you didn't know that."

"I bet you didn't know that, according to the Chinese waiter in the tavern here, Bien, that the ancient Chinese called ambergris 'Lung Sien Hiang.' The ancients believed that it was formed from the drooling of fierce dragons resting or sleeping on a rocky cliff near the sea. And you think you can tell stories! Put that one in your musket!"

"That's a wild story, Shanghai. I didn't think you would know about – or even be interested in such fables!"

"I've got a few others. Old Chinese tales."

"Another time," interjected Nathaniel. We'd better get some sleep so we're not tired tomorrow. Maybe we'll end up getting our own whale stories to tell!"

CHAPTER 29
AT SEA

Standing up in the whaleboat several miles out to sea and trying to aim the iron harpoon into the vulnerable part of the sperm whale's head, Nathaniel amazed the others with his unbelievable skill, fearlessness, and courage. The large whale looming in front of their whaleboat seemed like a relentless sea monster about to crush them. They didn't know that Nathaniel, at this decisive moment, if they could read his mind, didn't care whether he lived or died.

To Nathaniel, the whale was the personification of death which he was trying to eradicate, and in his own feverish mind, try to even the score. Whaleman and Shanghai Jim noticed the wild look on his face and his uncharacteristic muttering of a string of epithets almost to the point of screaming as he plunged the harpoon deep into the whale's head. Some crewmen were scrambling to secure the ties from the boat to the whale as Nathaniel furiously pushed the harpoon in further while others used sharp, metal-tipped lances to finish off the whale.

Whaleman and Shanghai Jim, too busy to analyze the reckless and bizarre actions of their friend, struggled to secure the whale to the boat and then row with the whale in tow toward shore. Nathaniel sat on the narrow bench at the bow, motionless, appearing dazed and trembling as if he had just awakened from a nightmare. Whaleman and

Shanghai Jim thought that they would question Nathaniel later about his boldness and erratic behavior as he fought and looked apparently into the face of death.

On shore, specialists skillfully separated the various parts of the sperm whale: blubber with its precious whale oil, which was destined for oil lamps, and the pale yellow whale sperm, which would all be used for making candles, ointments, and similar products, and the whalebone which would be carved into tools and utensils. The tail and fins, which were considered useless, unprofitable, and therefore expendable, were usually given to the Indian workers as part of their salary. The two parts, however, were used by Indians to make tools, decorative items, mats, and even clothing.

Since each whale was worth about $21,000, a considerable sum in 1769, the whale was therefore expertly stripped of every usable or sellable part. At that time in what was called the "Golden Age" of whaling, oil sold for at least 31 cents a gallon, sperm about 62 cents a gallon, and whalebone for more than $4.00 a pound. Buyers, sometimes before the whaling boats had even arrived on shore, haggled with company officials to offer the best competitive bids for each desired part of the whale.

The boats of Nathaniel's company, whose main base of operation was Sag Harbor, where its ships were moored, competed with the other companies' 15 whaling vessels also situated in the harbor. Many decades later, when whalers had to track the diminishing number of whales hundreds of miles south of Long Island and even around South America's Cape Horn, the whaling industry began to die.

But, in 1769, the whaling business was flourishing in the midst of increasing unalterable tension between the British soldiers and the colonial patriots - when both were on the brink of the seemingly inevitable American Revolution four years later.

CHAPTER 30
THE SPY

Both of Nathaniel's friends the next day decided not to question Nathaniel about his patently irrational and overly emotional behavior in harpooning the whale. They presumed that Nathaniel's pent-up emotion and frustration about the death of Arandel sought release in what he thought was his life-and-death struggle with his enemy – death. Whaleman and Shanghai didn't want to admit or discuss their innermost fear - that Nathaniel didn't want to live anymore. Fortunately, especially for Nathaniel, who again seemed to flirt with death on their next two whaling outings, they all survived the ordeal.

The trio decided in 1770 that they had made enough money to buy a local tavern – a venture much less strenuous and dangerous than whaling. The tavern, recently built, was bought from an old Dutchman who couldn't resist their generous offer. The combination pub and hotel with back rooms where customers, despite Nathaniel's objection, could pay for the hourly services of prostitutes, or as Whaleman called them, "full-bosomed ladies."

Nathaniel and Whaleman were content to lead quiet lives as the owners of a rustic, colonial inn, but Shanghai was still anxious about saving enough money to be able to return to his native Shanghai in northeast China. Unfortunately, Shanghai spent too much of his business earnings in enjoying the services, at cut-rate prices for owners, of the women in the back room and for his other less expensive craving – drinking whiskey or rum. Shanghai was still uncomfortable associating sexually with the occasionally available few Indian squaws, or even with the more numerous white women prostitutes.

"You should fancy one of those very pretty Indian squaws," Whaleman would advise Shanghai when Nathaniel wasn't around. "Or those Dutch and English waitresses here who work for us and who are willing and not married." But Shanghai felt he would only be comfortable with a woman who was Chinese and not a prostitute and who truly loved him despite "all my faults."

In 1770, it was evident that the British imposition of taxes and show of force was leading to a revolt by the American patriots. Much of the conflict occurred in Boston, eastern New Jersey, and Manhattan. The British occupation of Manhattan and a few parts of Long Island would last for years.

A formidable deterrent for the British was the undetermined loyalty of the Algonquin Indians on Long Island although it appeared likely that the Indians probably would side with the colonial patriots or "Whigs." The conflict even touched what was now named "Whaleman's Tavern" where "Minute Men" periodically met not only to discuss the oppressiveness of the British policies and the presence of British soldiers but also to formulate contingency military plans.

In September, 1775, five years later, the newly established Provincial Congress would order the disarmament of Loyalists or British sympathizers, and then their arrest if they posed a threat to the patriots. A few months later, the Continental Congress would order the arrest of suspected British loyalists who had congregated in what they thought was a safe haven – the far eastern part of Long Island.

The antagonistic events beginning in 1770 were unfortunately leading inexorably to the war between the British and the colonials. But, in the relatively halcyon days before open warfare, many citizens on the island, including Nathaniel, led a very satisfying, peaceful, and contented life.

One night in December, 1770, Nathaniel was sitting alone at a corner table of Whaleman's Tavern, basking in the warmth of the fireplace as the snow began to fall outside. He was waiting for his two best friends to join him.

"Pardon me, sir," said the tall and dignified gentleman, "am I speaking to Nathaniel Townsend?"

"Yes. And you sir, are?"

"My name for the time being doesn't matter. May I join you? I will take only a few minutes of your time."

"Of course, it would be my pleasure. Would you like a drink? Rum? Whiskey?"

"No, thank you. May I get to the point? I understand that you are very familiar with Indian ways and are quite skilled in using weapons such as the pistol, musket, knife, tomahawk, and even the bow and arrow? Skills, I would imagine, beyond those of the average man? Is that correct?"

"I would say so, sir, even if what I say sounds immodest. I learned all these weapons in…"

"Your ten years in Chief Tackapousha's village."

"Yes. How did you know that?"

"Be patient. I'll explain all in a moment. But first, I am told that you are a patriot and a completely trustworthy and honest person."

"I would hope so, sir. But why these questions? And who, may I ask again, are you?"

"Let me get to the reasons for my questions and in ascertaining your identity. I am Benjamin Tallmadge, a special aide to George Washington. It is almost certain that soon, perhaps in a year or two or more, General Washington, according to prominent colonial leaders, will be elevated to the position of Commander - in - Chief of the Continental Army. By then, he wants a spy system on Long Island set in place. Therefore, he has instructed me to inquire if you would accept a secret position as colonial Army scout and undercover spy. Your knowledge of the island and familiarity with the Indian tribes could be very helpful to Washington and to our cause in the future. Are you agreeable?"

"Of course. I have great admiration for him and for his leadership during the French and Indian War. And, from what I have heard, he is very sympathetic to the interests of the Indians here as well as elsewhere."

"That is true. Washington will be very pleased with your decision. In due time, we will work out your compensation which will be commensurate with such a potentially dangerous role which I will explain in due time."

"I am glad to be of service, Mr. Tallmadge, and I am honored that George Washington is interested in my services."

"You can thank Chief Tackapousha for that. I have spoken to the Chief for his advice and various recommendations, and he told me that he highly regards you as an honorable and patriotic young man as well as a distinguished warrior. He told me how you saved his village and why you are known throughout the island as the 'Golden Warrior.' I was very impressed with what he said, Mr. Townsend."

"Thank you, Mr. Tallmadge. If I may, did Chief Tackapousha say anything else?"

"No, except he kept calling you 'my son, Nathaniel.' He obviously has a great deal of respect and love for you."

Nathaniel looked away for a brief moment as painful visions of the past crossed his mind.

"Yes. I know. For ten years, he was my second father who… but that's another story."

"Is everything all right, Mr. Townsend? You look a bit pale… troubled."

"No, no. It is nothing. Everything's fine."

Tallmadge leaned closer to Nathaniel, and in a very low voice supplied him with the details he needed to know. As Washington's emissary left, Whaleman and Shanghai had entered the tavern, brushing off snowflakes from their heads and clothing.

"Who's the chap you were talking to just now, Nathaniel? If you don't mind us asking."

"A friend, Whaleman. I'll tell you about it tomorrow. Right now I have to get some sleep."

His two friends then went behind the bar, joked with the bartender, and then each poured a glass of whiskey.

"Good for the soul," remarked Whaleman as he quickly downed a second drink.

Leaving the tavern, Nathaniel didn't realize that the snow was descending more heavily since he was preoccupied with thinking about the new position just offered him and also the warm words Chief Tackapousha had said about him.

Just outside the front door among the snowflakes, he saw a shadowy figure that somehow seemed vaguely familiar. As his eyes became adjusted to the darkness, he saw that it looked like an Indian squaw.

"Do you not know me, Nathaniel? I am your sister, Martha."

CHAPTER 31
MARTHA

Nathaniel was speechless. His mind raced through a series of flashbacks as he tried to reconcile the image of the mature Indian squaw before him with that of his eight-year old sister, Martha. Could this really be his sister who suddenly disappeared from his life about twelve years ago?

Her voice sounded almost the same except it was deeper pitched and more womanly. Her short bearskin jacket covered a deerskin blouse and the top of her leggings which just touched her ankle-high leather boots - all of which were typical of what a squaw would wear in the winter. What used to be blonde curly hair, he noticed, was now obscured apparently by years of applying darkish bear grease and dyes. Her forehead revealed the traditional vermillion, or reddish-orange markings, which identified the Mohawk subtribe of the Iroquois who had settled in the upper New York colony.

"I am Martha, your sister. Do you not recognize me? It has been a long time. More than twelve years. I was afraid that you would not remember me. I thought I would never see you again. Oh, Nathaniel!"

"I can't believe it's you. I always regretted not staying to help you! Chief Tackapousha later told me that you probably were dead or kidnapped to serve some Iroquois warrior."

"The Chief was right. There's so much to tell. They tied me up and brought me to their Mohawk camp near the country that is named Canada. Oh, Nathaniel, I tried so many times to escape. Every day I used to think of our parents and you. That's what gave me hope."

In a burst of emotion, Nathaniel hugged her and cried, "It's been so long, Martha. I truly thought I would never see you again!"

Then she told him in a rush of words what she then felt compelled to say and which had been emotionally buried for so many years. "It was horrible. The Iroquois hilled our mother with a tomahawk right before my eyes. I saw the blood – all that blood on her blonde hair. I tried to run out the door, but another Brave grabbed me. I saw you frozen with fear, in shock. I didn't think you realized that I was being carried away by another Indian. You couldn't have helped me even if you wanted to. They then tied me up and put me in a wagon."

"You know, Martha, I think for a while I really was in shock and that I must have blocked out what happened. All I remember was going out the door, past the Indian perhaps holding you, or the other me – or maybe you were already gone - I'm not sure - and running as fast as I could down the street. Later, I regretted not trying to look for you and our father."

"You did the right thing, Nathaniel. You were only eight-years old. Like me. I was taken out of the store actually before you ran out. Good thing they didn't kill you as they did so many others. You couldn't have helped me. And…and…tell me – what happened to our father? Is he still alive?"

"No, Martha…Chief Tackapousha, the Indian Chief who helped me, later told me that our father also was killed and that he was found dead lying next to our mother."

Martha started to sob, and Nathaniel held her more tightly. "I suspected it, Nathaniel, but I didn't want to believe it. I always hoped that perhaps…" And then she couldn't talk anymore.

"You can tell me later more about what happened to you, Martha. It's very cold here. Come inside with me to where it is warm. I also want you to meet my friends."

Nathaniel held her by the hand and led her inside to the light and warmth inside the inn. "Gentlemen, I would like to introduce you to my sister, Martha."

Whaleman and Shanghai Jim, wide-eyed and stunned, stared at the dark-haired white squaw holding hands with Nathaniel.

CHAPTER 32

REACQUAINTED

At first, Martha stayed with Nathaniel for much of the next two years in his little cabin. After a week, she had shed her Mohawk color markings, cleansed her hair and, with her brother's help, bought some new clothing. Happy to be reunited with Nathaniel and appreciative of his kindness, she did all the cooking and cleaning. When he thought she had acclimated to her new existence and was ready to discuss in detail what happened to her since he last saw her, he brought up the subject.

She described how the Mohawk had carried her to a wagon where she was tied up and eventually transported across the East and Hudson Rivers and northward to a Mohawk settlement at the northwestern bend of the Mohawk River. Two other white women, both in their late teens, were also captured and put with her in the same Indian lodge. They were forced to do many of the manual chores such as cleaning utensils, washing clothes, and tending to and gathering the garden vegetables which they were taught how to cook. For five years, she was left alone until the son of the Chief took a liking to her, when she was thirteen years old.

"Then he...he...he...."

"It's all right, Martha, I understand. You were only thirteen.

You couldn't help it. You were a prisoner. He was stronger than you were." He held her close to him. "You don't have to say anymore. I understand. It's all in the past."

"I have to get it out of my system, Nathaniel. It was awful. He…he… assaulted me and then forced me to become one of his two wives. Nobody could help me. I felt so ashamed…so degraded. I couldn't believe this was happening to me! And I was only thirteen and all alone! Oh, Nathaniel!"

"It's all right now. It's over. You're with me. I'll take care of you."

"At least I was fortunate that I didn't have any children. I tried to escape many times, but they always caught me. They didn't punish me except to give me more work to do. And they kept an even closer eye on me."

"How did you manage to finally escape, Martha?"

"I was very lucky. For some reason, perhaps sexual or for me to do the cooking, the Chief's son brought me with him to Manhattan for a big annual meeting - something to do with the British and the colonists. Perhaps he also didn't trust leaving me alone with his younger brother who was constantly paying too much attention to me."

She took a deep breath. "One night, the two Braves guarding me in this little building between the two rivers got drunk, and I managed to slip by them. By the time they realized I was gone, I had walked to the East River. There, a kindly old Dutch gentleman felt sorry for me and agreed, for the little wampum I had in my belt, to row me across the water."

"How, then, did you find me, Martha? It's a big island."

"The Dutch man directed me to Canarsies Town where a stranger, the first person I talked to, told me about you. I was surprised that he knew about you."

"Know him," he said. "Everybody knows him. He's a hero. He helped save Chief Tackapousha's village. They called him the 'Golden Warrior' because of his blond hair and how he killed half the attacking Narragansetts himself."

"I asked him where I could find you in the chance that he might know."

"I know where," he said. "Probably at Whaleman's Tavern. I was there myself last week. It's only a few miles northeast of here."

"He not only described you to me but also gave me directions, and I walked for hours to get here. It's fortunate that you are very famous, my hero brother, or I may not have been able to find you!"

She looked at him. "Do you know what I was thinking when I first saw you in the snow that night? I was thinking of the little boy who wanted to play spin the tops instead of playing with my dolls. Then I saw how big you were and how you changed and how happy I was to see you again!"

In time, after Martha regained her spirited nature, she volunteered to work as a waitress at the tavern. Nathaniel at first was reluctant because he was fearful that some of the customers, especially those who had too much to drink, might try to manhandle her, pinch her bottom, or make lurid suggestions. But she said she could handle herself and, if not, would gladly try finding another job. True to her word, she handled herself quite well and after many months earned not only Whaleman's admiration but also his growing affection for her.

It wasn't before long that Whaleman, the tavern's official manager, and Martha began socializing and becoming serious about each other. Nathaniel noticed how well Martha and Whaleman got along together and how happy his sister was since she started working as a waitress. Then, one evening in the tavern in July, 1773, Whaleman sat down next to Nathaniel who was just beginning his Shepherd's Pie supper. "Can I talk to you for a minute, Nathaniel?"

"Of course, and why are you asking me? You usually just sit down and start talking. Anything wrong?"

"No, just the opposite. You know that Martha and I have been seeing each other for a while now?"

"How could I not notice it, Whaleman? You're over at my cabin almost every other night talking with her sometimes until all hours!"

"Yes, yes, I know. Sorry. But to get to the point…The thing is that Martha and I are in love, and since you're the closest that she has to a father, I'm asking for your permission to marry her."

"Whaleman, this is not unexpected, and I appreciate your showing her and me the respect of asking for my approval. You're a fine, decent, honorable man…a little talkative and boisterous at times…but if I ever had to pick a husband for her, it would certainly be you. Of course, I approve. And my congratulations to you both!"

Later, Martha hugged and kissed him so many times that he had to beg her to stop. In the next few weeks, the four of them, which included Shanghai Jim who didn't want to be excluded, finalized plans for the wedding and subsequent small reception in the tavern.

There were two regrets dimming her joy: that her parents couldn't see her get married, and the other was sadness concerning Nathaniel. When her brother finally was able to tell her about him and Arandel, she couldn't stop crying. For several nights she cried herself to sleep because she thought of the hurt Nathaniel must have endured and knew now why, at times, he would unexplainably become silent and sad.

The impending marriage in 1773 of Whalemen and Martha made Nathaniel think more about Jessie who had befriended him and Arandel in the years before she died. Jessie, he later realized, had always reminded him of Arandel. They both had the same happy smile, exuberant personality, teasing sense of humor, and love of nature. He knew that Jessie once had affectionate feelings toward him as he did in his own way for her. Would there be a second chance for him?

Nathaniel went to see Jessie and they both soon realized their deep affection for each other. After some soul-searching and Nathaniel's making peace with the past, they acknowledged their love for each other. Martha and Whaleman were delighted to be told that Nathaniel's wedding to Jessie would probably occur in the following year, 1774.

Chapter 33
Happiness

For most of 1774, Nathaniel slept without sad memories haunting his dreams. He awoke each day refreshed and exhilarated and always remembering Jessie's warm embrace and kisses and her joy when he asked her to marry him months ago. Even though he knew he would eventually marry Jessie, he had postponed the wedding date several times for reasons he didn't want to admit to himself.

He started one morning to sing part of a colonial love song, "All in a Misty Morning," something that he hardly ever did and which surprised him. He also began thinking how he would have to prepare the cabin when Jessie eventually moved in with him after their marriage. Some of the parting gifts given to him by Chief Tackapousha and his tribal members in 1769 would have to be relocated to inside the wood shed in back of the cabin. His three rooms, despite their large size, were cluttered with knives, tomahawks, pistols, muskets, an assortment of bows, and quartz and antler-tipped arrows. Even the Massapequan squaws had given him many handmade blankets, rugs, and ceramic pottery.

One large gift which he could never remove or discard was a large ceramic vase given to him when Arandel and he were eighteen years old. On the vessel, made by Arandel, in large red and yellow colors, she had painted TO MY GOLDEN WARRIOR.

Many a night he had tried to relieve his anguish by staring at the vase which was her special personal gift given to him on the day of his eighteenth birthday. That night, after he had asked Jessie to marry him, for a brief moment, the unpleasant memories had returned, but then the thought of Jessie, whom he would probably marry in late 1774, obscured these dark thoughts.

On June 15, 1774, with a sense of well-being and cheerfulness, he shaved, bathed in his large oak tub, and dressed. He put on his fringed deerskin jacket and leggings, racoon cap, and soft moccasins. He then slipped his long knife into its hip sheath, placed his pistol inside his jacket pocket, and later would put his musket on a sling attached to the side of his horse tied outside. In case he met any renegade Indians or hostile British patrol redcoats, he was prepared, if necessary, to defend himself. He knew that the British troops would be suspicious of and challenge anyone so heavily armed and travelling without purpose in the middle of nowhere.

He obviously couldn't tell the British that he was a scout since he would be considered the enemy who was employed by the colonials. If his true role as a spy were uncovered, he could be imprisoned or shot. Nathaniel had figured that if he were stopped, he would say that he was a tavern owner who was hunting for game.

Even though it was unlikely – even after the American Revolution had started - that he would encounter British soldiers anywhere except in parts of Manhattan and on the extreme edges of the island, he was prepared for any eventuality. Once several intoxicated British troops stopped him near Cold Spring Harbor and would have unnecessarily shot him if their sergeant-major hadn't intervened and decided that he was harmless. In these revolutionary, dangerous, and volatile times, he knew that anything could happen.

His assignment that day on June 15, 1774, was to determine the number of British troops who had sailed from New York Harbor east to Sag Harbor. According to some of Nathaniel's former fellow whalers, the British troops were investigating, and possibly seizing, the Cook Company's whaling ships. Some of the whaling ships, manned by unauthorized colonial sailors or "pirates," had previously attacked and plundered British vessels moored at the northern tip of Manhattan.

The report was that the rogue whalers, for profit and not for patriotism, had overwhelmed the unsuspecting British soldiers on the supply ships. The mercenary pirates confiscated British firearms, clothing, liquor, and valuable whale parts the Redcoats had themselves stolen from the colonials. Also, some patriots who had been captured and imprisoned in one of the British vessels being used as a prison ship, were freed. Many British sailors and redcoats died in the early morning sneak attack. Upset at the illegal assault and criminality which impugned the American whaling industry and its honest workers, Nathaniel had only contempt for the villainous colonial pirates.

Just before leaving the cabin, he debated the practicality of bringing his musket. The musket was not always reliable when speed was essential in times of emergencies because it took too long to load and fire.

Suddenly, a loud booming noise coming from his front door startled him. It couldn't be Martha or his two friends since they always knocked gently or called out his name. With pistol in one hand, he slowly pushed aside the simple locking device and slowly opened the creaking front and only door.

CHAPTER 34
THE MONTAUK

Standing, and with twenty other warriors seated on their horses behind him, was Chief Pharoah of the Montauk Indians subtribe. Nathaniel, unafraid, stared at this tall and young imposing figure whose dark brown face seemed strangely familiar.

Nathaniel knew immediately that the man before him had to be a Chief. In addition to his commanding presence, he wore a brightly-colored wampum belt with white and sepin feathers in his hair which was without a scalp lock. Around his neck was a white and black beaded necklace, the traditional sign of peace usually worn in 1774 by an Indian of great importance - such as a Chief, son or daughter of a Chief, or medicine man.

"Do not be afraid, Nathaniel. We will not harm you."

Nathaniel wasn't fearful since he had noticed the necklace of peace, the calm demeanor of the stranger, and the knowledge that an Indian Chief with harmful intentions usually would not be foolish enough to be vulnerable to attack by getting off his horse. Nathaniel knew personally many of the island's Indian Chiefs, but this one's youthful and somewhat familiar face was unknown and puzzling. And, thought Nathaniel, how did this unknown Chief know his name?

"Do you not remember me, you of the Massapequans and

Chief Tackapousha's son, the one he calls 'The Golden Warrior'?"

Nathaniel kept staring and trying to determine why the face was so familiar. His wampum belt, made from the valued purple part of the whelk or snail shell, further suggested his affluence and high standing.

"I see you do not know me. I am Chief Pharoah of the Montauks. I thought it was likely that you would not remember me since much time has passed, since we last met, my friend."

Nathaniel wondered why he called him "friend." He knew that the Montauks, the most easterly Algonquin subtribe, had the unusual tradition of naming their Chiefs after the pharaohs of Egypt (until 1832, when the last Montauk pharaoh died).

"It was many moons ago when you helped me, an Indian and a complete stranger -in fact, a young boy - by attending to my musket wound. My father, the Chief, and I were seeking revenge against evil white settlers who cheated and killed some of our warriors in Montauk territory as they were also trying to do against other white settlers as well as some peaceful Indians further west in the land of the Merricks. It is sad that some innocent white settlers in the Merricks were killed as were some of our Braves who had sought revenge. Some renegades – I believe that is the word you use – helped some of the evil white attackers in the Merricks."

"My God. I do remember now. You're a bit taller and older now! You certainly grew up very fast since then. Then it wasn't a British - inspired renegade attack as we all thought then! I believe, if I'm not mistaken, that the attack happened about four years or so ago. You certainly grew up since then. I do remember helping a young, frightened Indian Brave by bandaging his bleeding arm. And that was you! It is hard to believe."

"Yes, that is true. You helped me. I thought you were going to kill me. But you did not. You took care of my wound. I have never forgotten your face - and your kindness."

Chief Pharaoh smiled at Nathaniel. "As you might know, when my father, a very old man died, I became, with honor but much sadness, the Chief at a young age. I also had learned how to speak your English language which has been very helpful to me. The great Chief Tackapousha, your Indian father, told me that you learned our Algonquin language when you lived with his tribe. I am speaking to you now in your white man's tongue so that all I say will be very clear to you. May I enter your home, my friend?"

"Yes, yes, of course." Nathaniel was still recalling the memory of that terrible attack and of his helping a teen-age boy who apparently was trying just a short time ago to be a warrior sooner than he should have.

"Now, Nathaniel Townsend, I have come, in part, to return your kindness to me. But, there is also a very serious matter which I have already discussed with Chief Tackapousha. He said that if any man can be trusted, it is you. It is also of importance personally to your General George Washington and your fight with the British."

"Really. What does it have to do with George Washington?"

"We also have many spies, and we know that General Washington hired you to be a scout but actually a spy for the colonists, a job you've done for a few years now. Chief Tackapousha also told us this. Is that not true?"

"Yes. That is so, Chief Pharoah. Chief Tackapousha would never lie."

"Times have changed. At one time, many years ago, we were friends with the British who protected us from the more powerful Indians in Connecticut, the Narragansetts, who kept asking us for more and more tribute. In return, my father gave the British much whale blubber and whale oil which they loaded onto their ships docked near

Southampton before they set sail for Manhattan."

Nathaniel had flinched at the mention of the name Narragansetts.

"Does all of this make you sad, my friend? Your face shows disturbance."

"No. No, continue, Chief Pharaoh. It is nothing. Please continue."

"It was also humil...humiliating...for Montauks who a century ago were known as the most powerful tribe on the island. But those times are past. And it is becoming more and more a white man's world. It is a sad thing that I am able to see all sides - that of the British, the Indians, and the settlers. But in my time the British have now not been kind to the Algonquins – as well as the settlers - on the island."

"But you spoke of General Washington. What is his concern in all of this?"

"I will tell you plainly. The British and one Indian tribe here are planning to kill your great Chief, Washington. He is coming here in August of this year, 1774, to meet with the Chiefs of all the thirteen tribes to get their support in the fight against the British soldiers."

"It can't be. To kill Washington? And one treacherous tribe here is against us! That is hard to believe. I used to know all the tribes. What tribe is that, Chief Pharaoh?

"It is a very small - very small group of Algonquins who broke off from the Canarsies. I will tell you more in a few minutes. Be patient, Nathaniel."

"Of course. I know that General Washington has fought against the British in Manhattan, now controlled by the British, and in New Jersey. I didn't know the General was also interested in enlisting the support of the tribes here on Long Island. The British, I know, however, are very interested in the sheep, cattle, whale products, and all the other food sources here."

"That is also true. General Washington wants to con...confront the British by getting our help and also to protect us. The British are very strong, Nathaniel."

"Which I know. Isn't it dangerous for him to come here? In a time of war and away from his soldiers?"

"He will be guarded, and he will come in secret at the right time. You may not know that this will not be the first time he has come here. He has met before with Chief Tackapousha. I believe that was after you left his village. Chief Tackapousha suggested that I come to their meeting since we have the most warriors and are concerned with the heavy hostile British movement in the eastern part of the island."

"You're right. I never knew that, Chief Pharaoh. How did you learn of this plot?"

"From a former loyal Montauk who went to live with that evil tribe when he married one of their squaws. He told us, and we sent the information to the General via a special messenger."

"Why does not General Washington send someone in his place to speak to the Chiefs of the thirteen tribes? It would be much safer."

"He told us, Nathaniel, that he wants all of the thirteen Chiefs to know that his interest in us is so strong and important that he will personally meet with the Chiefs and show no fear in doing so. He is a very brave man and a great leader."

"I agree. So he'll really be here in August?"

"Yes, in August, in this year, 1774, as I have said, in a meeting in the great lodge of your Indian father, Chief Tackapousha. Chief Tackapousha is also a brave Chief and, as you know, of much stature in the Indian world. He is also a very smart man, Nathaniel. He is the one who developed the plan to safe...safeguard your General and who suggested that you be present at the meeting to protect Washington."

"I am pleased that both of you have confidence in me. I will do everything I can to help and protect General Washington and my... my...Chief Tackapousha."

"Yes, I know, Nathaniel. You can say what is the truth. You do consider Chief Tackapousha your second father. And it is proper for you to say it. He has told us many times about you, the 'Golden Warrior,' and about Arandel. A sad story. He knows his daughter would have approved of your participation and would have wanted you to help. He said that Arandel was very proud of you and that you loved each other...Let me tell you, now, if I may, of the plan."

CHAPTER 35

SECRET MEETING

Nathaniel listened intently as Chief Pharaoh revealed how Washington would be secretly transported at night from somewhere near the vicinity of New York to Chief Tackapousha's lodge thirty miles to the east. The wooded and sinuous route will be one not easily discovered so it is highly unlikely that it will be known to the British or even the evil tribe. Washington and his guards will be in plain clothes and will covertly be guided by some of Chief Tackapousha's Braves.

"The General will be escorted by the same number of guards when he, Chief Tackapousha, and I met last year to discuss the details of what Washington believed would be a very important meeting. He wanted the Long Island Indians to unite with him against the British who had gradually been infiltrating the island. We have contacted all the Algonquin Chiefs, obviously excluding the Iroquois and their subtribe, Mohawks, who are aligned, we believe, with the British and the one evil tribe."

"Will the lodge be prepared to hold all the Chiefs? When I left, it needed many repairs, Chief Pharaoh."

"You are right, Nathaniel. When you were there it was, as you know, part of what was called Fort Neck and was in great need of repairs. The Chief has already been rebuilding it."

"That will be a good thing, Chief. The fort is a very historical place. It was a refuge, as you know, where local peaceful Indians in the past protected themselves against possible foes. In 1653, Chief Tackapousha told me, it was the site of the bloodiest battle ever fought on the island. The British, under Captain John Underhill, killed many Indians and destroyed most of the fort because of white settlers fearing violence from the territory's Indians who actually were peacefully inhabiting the fort."

Chief Tackapousha, Nathaniel learned, planned to restore the four-sided log building to its original size: 60 feet long, 25 feet wide, and 20 feet high. When both were twelve years old, Nathaniel remembered Arandel telling him about the lodge and one-time fort. They had played many times in the remaining structure of the old building.

"It was a very bad time, Nathaniel," Arandel had said. "My father says that, at least, the women and children in 1653 didn't have to fight. They were sent to Squaw Island in the Great Bay until the fighting was over."

"Yes, as you say, I am aware of that story, Nathaniel," said Chief Pharoah. "Perhaps, now, it can again serve an even better purpose."

Nathaniel looked at Chief Pharoah with even more respect. For such a very young Indian Chief, probably about twenty years old, he spoke very wisely and with a maturity beyond his years.

"Now, Nathaniel, let me tell you how we think you can help. We want you to be in the meeting room with us to protect Washington. Weapons, for obvious reasons, will not be allowed, except in your case. You can conceal a knife, a pistol, or whatever you prefer. The Chiefs will be told that you will observe them to make sure they follow this rule: no weapons. You should pay much attention to this one evil Chief. We do not trust him. The Chiefs will also be told that, in case there is a problem with interpreting some Algonquin words, if need be, you will help. That is another reason to have you there. Because of your honorable reputation and fame as the great 'Golden Warrior,' the Chiefs will think that your presence there will en…enhance the importance of the occasion even more."

"I am honored that you and they may think so. I will do whatever I can to help. But, now tell me. Who is this evil Chief that you speak of? It is hard for me to believe that any Algonquin Chief can have such dishonorable intentions."

"Chief Ohenton, Nathaniel, is a man of great ambition and greed. At one time, he wished to be selected as the Chief Sachem of all the island Sachems, but he was rebuffed at the great Council Meeting. We have learned that the English became aware of his dis… dissatisfaction with other Chiefs and his thirst for power and wealth. The British, we understand, offered him much money, in wampum and English coin, and all the land he wanted. The deceitful British, speaking falsely, promised him all the land he desired when the British defeated Washington and his soldiers and, of course, all the Indian tribes, on Paumanok."

"Why don't you kill him now before he can do anything?"

"We have to be certain. We don't want to upset the other Chiefs if we can't show definite proof of the treachery of this Chief and, as you say, his bad intentions. They will then see him also as an obvious enemy. And they will realize how powerful Washington is in dealing with this Chief and how determined he is in protecting and uniting them. It should not be too difficult since the Indians, as well as most of the white men here, do not like or trust the British. The British are despised because of their unfair taxes, and for stealing our cattle, our sheep, our horses, and even the result of our labor after we have killed the mighty whale."

"I agree, Chief Pharoah, that the meeting will show Washington's bravery as well as his support of the Indians. It will be good for the morale of all of us - Indians and settlers - and for the defense of our island."

"Your words are loyal and well spoken, my friend. Chief Tackapousha spoke true words when he spoke highly of your character and loyalty. But now let me tell you the details of our plan."

Even though they were alone, Chief Pharaoh looked around the room nervously as if his words could somehow reach the ears of the enemy.

CHAPTER 36
THE PLAN

Chief Pharaoh, taking a deep breath and speaking very slowly, looked intently at Nathaniel as if to determine his reactions to what he was saying.

The Chief unfolded the plan. As Washington was being safely escorted to Chief Tackapousha's lodge, three hundred friendly Braves would be hiding in the woods one hundred yards north of it. The British Redcoats and Chief Ohenton's War Party, numbering about 200, according to Chief Pharaoh's information, would attack from the south. The attackers would race through the camp and eliminate anyone in their way. A small contingent of Chief Ohenton's Narreckhewicks would be assigned to burn the wigwams to demonstrate the superiority and destructive power of the assailants and to serve as a lesson to those who would oppose the British and Chief Ohenton.

"Who will be the Braves waiting in the north woods, Chief Pharaoh?"

"They will mostly be warriors from the Massapequas, Montauks, and Shinnecock subtribes. There are a few from the other subtribes except those of or near Chief Ohenton's village. It wouldn't be worth the risk if Chief Ohenton found out about the plan ahead of time from the nearby Canarsies and other subtribes. The Canarsies

Chief was sworn to secrecy, and after being told of the plan, was willing to send many Braves to repay Chief Tackapousha for the two times he helped save their village. But, his generous offer, under the circumstances, was declined. It was, and still is, very difficult to keep this plan a secret, but we think we have done so and will succeed. We have had many meetings discussing the plan, Nathaniel."

Mentioning again Arandel's comment about the tragic slaughter of many Indians by the British in 1653, Nathaniel showed compassionate concern about the safety of the Indian women and children in Chief Tackapousha's village.

"I see you are concerned about Arandel's story which her father also reminded me of. Do not worry about them, Nathaniel. The women and children will be brought safely to an area near the Great Bay where they will be taken care of by the Matinecocks."

"Fine. But how will we know when the enemy will be close enough to the meeting place so that we can surprise them by attacking them first? I assume that is the plan?"

"Yes, Nathaniel. We know the routes they are taking. After the Redcoats cross the East River, they will try to make people believe that they are on a routine patrol. The Redcoats and Chief Ohenton's Braves will take different trails until they meet about two miles south of Chief Tackapousha's village. We have a number of scouts, hidden of course, who will relay by various means the enemy's progress to us."

"It sounds like a very good plan. I am not familiar with the this Chief Ohenton. He is one of the Chiefs that I have never met. He must have come into power after I left Chief Tackapousha's camp. It is too bad that we have to deal with such a treacherous person."

"That, as I said before, will also be your job - to watch and observe him as soon as he enters the lodge. He is a very dangerous man. A violent one. When the Canarsies selected someone else as

Chief two years ago, he was so enraged that he, with his followers, separated from the Canarsies, and settled in a small plain near a hill called Narreckhewicks on the other side of the valley. His temper and outbursts at island Council meetings are known by all the other Chiefs. You would have known this, Nathaniel, if, as you said, you still lived in Chief Tackapousha's camp."

"That is true, Chief Pharoah. I presume that the British think by killing Washington, a year after the war started, they will shorten the war by easily defeating the patriots. They must be very desperate to attempt such a daring assassination!"

"We think so. But they are very serious and very determined. Our informant tells us that the plot to kill General Washington came not from General William Cooper, the British Commanding General here, but from the King of England, King George himself! We heard that he does not have all his senses. The rumor is that he is — what you say - mentally unbalanced. He will be very disappointed when he learns that his plot has failed!"

Chief Pharoah discussed a few more details, drank his third cup of whiskey, and then took his leave, completely satisfied of Nathaniel's support of the plan and his willingness to take part.

After he left, Nathaniel was silent for a few minutes. Then he looked at the large pottery vase given to him by Arandel and thought, "If only Arandel were here. She would have been so proud of me...my Arandel... Arandel."

CHAPTER 37
DAYS BEFORE

Three days before the arrival of General Washington for the meeting on August 24, 1774, Nathaniel became very anxious about succeeding in his role of protecting him from the unpredictable Chief Ohenton. Nathaniel had the advantage of being the only participant who would be armed with knife and pistol, but he was still concerned about what could happen - the unexpected.

He was glad that day, August 21, to relax at a picnic arranged by Jessie in a glade near his cabin. Even though Jessie was always aware of Nathaniel's sensitivity about Arandel, including his sadness at saying or hearing her name, she forgot that the day of the picnic would have been Arandel's twenty - sixth birthday. Last year on that day, Jessie had noticed that Nathaniel had been very moody and withdrawn. It was too late now to reschedule the picnic so she hoped that Nathaniel wouldn't notice, especially since he seemed to be preoccupied with apparently some other matter.

"You seem to be in a pensive mood, my dear Nathaniel. Is anything troubling you?"

"No, Jessie. No. Don't be concerned. It is nothing. My thoughts are mainly about our wedding later this year and our future together." I promise not to postpone it again!"

"Yes. I feel the same way. I think about the wedding all the time. My father, bless his soul, is giving me a wonderful personal gift – a beautiful, flowery short gown. I picked it out. You will be pleased, Nathaniel."

"I like what you are wearing now. You are exceptionally beautiful Jessie," said Nathaniel as she blushed. He looked at her trim little figure, her white linen blouse, and blue wool blouse covered with a yellow-bordered pink apron. Because of the coolness in the air, she wore a woman's thin doublet over her blouse but underneath wore only one petticoat. The slight breeze ruffled her brown hair, and the sunlight seemed to make her blue eyes glisten. In what probably was a genetic oddity, he was always amazed that Arandel, unlike most Algonquin women, had clear, blue and not brown eyes. Chief Tackapousha had told him once that he also was baffled by her having blue eyes since everyone in his family line, as far as he knew, had brown eyes.

Nathaniel was dressed in his usual attire: light buckskin jacket, white cotton shirt, leggings, and white stockings. His coonskin hat, which he preferred instead of the more fashionable three – cornered felt hat, was lying by his side. They were both wearing soft, leather moccasins, which as Nathaniel knew, were of a type originally designed centuries before by the Algonquins. They both preferred moccasins instead of the traditional unshaped shoes with straight soles.

As Jessie placed the small mutton sandwiches, sweet potatoes, corn bread, and jug of cold cider on the blanket, Nathaniel's mind wandered. Was anything vulnerable about the plan, including secrecy? Was there enough protection for Washington? Would their scouts carefully monitor the routes taken by both enemy groups in case they took a different direction? Would he be able to handle any unforeseen eventuality at the meeting? Chief Pharoah had warned him several times about the deceptive and treacherous nature of Chief Ohenton. Would he be able to handle any unexpected situation that might occur?

"As you know, Nathaniel, my father is happy to have the wedding celebration at your tavern. He wondered, however, why the wedding was delayed several times and why we're getting married a little later than we planned, but he's still happy. Whaleman, Shanghai, and you were so kind in having the reception in the tavern – without charge. They said that you wouldn't mind since you were a partner who was getting married. Whaleman didn't actually say 'partner.' First, Whaleman had said 'poor fool,' and then he laughed. He apologized for his humorous remark, but he cheered up when I said he had a wonderful sense of humor!"

"That sounds just like Whaleman. Making sport of everything. I don't know how my sister puts up with him and his jests!"

"Because she loves him, Nathaniel. They are very suited for each other. I have to admit that Whaleman and Shanghai Jim are truly very agreeable and generous friends of yours. We can use the first floor of the inn for the party, and they said, as you also agreed, that there'll be no charge for the food and liquor. They're wonderful wedding gifts!" Generous of you, too, my sweetheart, since you're also an owner!"

"I want our wedding to be perfect, Jessie.. And you know how I feel about them. They are my two very good, kind, and faithful friends."

"You all made my father very happy. He always liked you, and he is well pleased that he will have to pay practically nothing for his daughter's wedding!"

"You're father's a very good, gentle man, Jessie. We're glad he is content. He reminds me of Chief Tackapousha. They're both about the same height and build, and they both have had daughters…" Words seemed to desert him as memories of Arandel returned.

She quickly changed the subject. "It's too bad my mother didn't live long enough to see me married. She also would have been so happy. She probably would have insisted on making my wedding gown!"

"What's that you have there, Jess? It looks like meat sandwiches and cider and…"

"It's one of your favorites. You must recognize it. It's lima beans and green corn mixed and heated, as you know, in the same pot. And what you also like - corn bread."

"That's very nice of you, Jessie. I got used to succotash and corn bread when I lived with the Indians. In fact, many times I had helped plant and pick the beans and corn. I haven't had it in a long time. It's very sweet and thoughtful of you. Thanks, Jess."

"Did I also tell you that my father is going to provide one of his cows for the wedding dinner? Whaleman said he would be happy to cook and then cut it up."

"He likes using his hands, the old codger!"

"Now, Nathaniel. Be nice. He's only seven years older than you and your sister. You talk as though he were an old man."

"You're right. He's a decent old…young fellow, I must say. By the way, you'd better tell your father to hide his cows and sheep."

"Why is that?"

"The British, since the war started in 1773, have occasionally been raiding island farms and seizing as many horses, cows, and sheep as they can. They use the cows and sheep to feed their soldiers. Chief Tackapousha once told me when I was about thirteen or fourteen that there were then probably at least 100,000 cows and even more sheep on the island. I said kiddingly to him, 'I hope you don't want me to count them.'

He smiled, turned to Arri…Arandel…and said, 'You better

teach him to count more than to ten!' Hardly anyone knew he had a sense of humor!"

Nathaniel hesitated for a moment. "I have to admit that the Chief was a very intelligent, visionary man whose view of the future, as he said many times, included the decline of the Long Island Indian tribes. He said that soon there would be so many settlers that they would outnumber the Indians and ultimately deprive them of their land and centuries - old heritage of earning a living through hunting, fishing, and planting. Chief Tackapousha believed that his people earned the right to the land because they settled here thousands of years ago and that they had exclusively ruled the island, sometimes not peacefully, until the last century, the 1600's, until the Dutch, English, and some German settlers arrived. In the early days, which to him was the 1600's, each subtribe had more than four hundred members. Today, except for a few tribes, such as the Massapequas, Montauks, and Shinnecocks, most Chiefs are leaders of about only one or two hundred tribesmen. Quite a difference, Jessie."

"You sound like a spokesman for the Indian cause, Nathaniel. It is obviously because you spent the last ten of your first eighteen years living with the Algonquins."

"It could be that at one time, Jessie, I almost thought I was an Indian and would forever remain one. But that seems like such a long time ago. Everything changes…everything. But, for you and me, it is a beginning – a beginning, I know, of a long and happy life."

CHAPTER 38
MISSION: KILL WASHINGTON

On the early morning of August 24, 1774, the English troops were close to joining the War Party of Narreckhewicks at a designated point two miles south of Chief Tackapousha's village. The British officers were intent on accomplishing their objective which, they theorized, would destroy the morale of the Patriots and lead to undisputed victory - and therefore an early end of the American Revolution.

The combined enemy forces intended to strike swiftly. The Indians would sweep through the village, burn the wigwams, and indiscriminately kill all of the probably still sleeping inhabitants. The British would storm the lodge and murder all the chieftains, except one, and do the same to the object of their mission - General Washington. If necessary, and if warranted by any unforeseen circumstances, it would be Chief Ohenton's responsibility to assassinate Washington.

As the tribal chiefs filed into the lodge at different times, Nathaniel looked for Chief Ohenton who had been thoroughly described to him by Chief Tackapousha and Chief Pharoah. Even if he hadn't been given a description of Chief Ohenton, he might still have noticed the strangeness of the sullen-faced sachem of medium height who talked to no one and who seemed anxious to sit quickly at the front table. He and the others had been screened and then admitted after being identified and approved by Chief Tackapousha himself.

A cordon of trusted Washington guards had been stationed around the lodge with a smaller security contingent near the north woods. The guards surrounding the lodge were advised that if there were an attack, hundreds of defenders would quickly rush from the northern woods to aid them.

At the appropriate time, Washington, preceded by Chief Tackapousha, had secretly entered the lodge. Behind Washington were Nathaniel and Benjamin Green, the General's aide-de-camp. Washington walked slowly down the aisle between the chairs and tables. Green had been assigned to verify the attendance of the Chiefs and had rehearsed the pronunciation of their names with Nathaniel and Chief Tackapousha. When he read the names, Green would be at the podium between Washington, on his right, and Chief Tackapousha, to his left. Nathaniel would be placed behind Green who would sit next to him after he read the names.

This would be the first time Nathaniel had actually seen and been this close to General Washington. How Arandel, he thought, would have been overjoyed at his being part of this historic occasion which was made possible by her father. She probably would have tried without success to attend the meeting. She would have been so proud – so proud of him - he kept thinking.

Nathaniel, awed by the sight of the General, saw him conferring with Chief Tackapousha and Green. Washington and Nathaniel were similar in some respects. They were both tall, with Nathaniel being taller by two inches than the six - foot colonial leader. If one had the opportunity to compare each one, he would have noted that they both exhibited similar qualities of calmness, confidence, and extreme self - control.

Because of his legendary status as one of the heroes of the French and Indian War and as Commander-in-Chief of the colonial forces, Washington's presence mesmerized and fascinated the tribal leaders except for one. After Green made a few very brief introductory remarks, first in simple Algonquin and then in English, he read the names of the Tribes alphabetically, and their Chiefs: Canarsies, Corchaugs, Manhassets, Massapequas, Matinecocks, Merricks, Montauks, Nissequogues, Rockaways, Secatogues, Selaukets, Shinnecocks, and Unechaugs. After reading the name of the subtribe Canarsies, Green had added "and their neighbors, the Narreckhewicks."

Since he had been covertly observing Chief Ohenton, he had noticed that when the Chief's name was mentioned, he moved his right hand underneath his gaudily decorated jacket as if to reassure himself of something hidden there. Nathaniel suspected that perhaps he was concealing, contrary to the rule, something - possibly a dagger or pistol or some other weapon.

CHAPTER 39

A CLOSE CALL

On a signal from the British commander, the hostile Braves in the very early morning stormed through the village, burning wigwams with fire arrows but too late realized that the settlement was deserted.

The British, also not realizing that the camp had been emptied, rushed within almost one hundred yards of the lodge when they saw the surprising sight of hundreds of Indians on horseback rushing toward them. Expecting little or no resistance, the Redcoats had just dismounted and had moved in horizontal formation quickly toward the lodge and with muskets and bayonets at the ready. By the time some of the Redcoats had fired and then re-loaded their muskets, they had been overwhelmed by the defenders.

In the lodge, the Chiefs heard the tumult and were not only startled but fearful since they had no weapons and were unaware of the defensive plan.

When none of the Redcoats or his Braves stormed through the door, Chief Ohenton assumed the worst. He believed that for some unknown reason, the assault apparently had failed. As the other Chiefs were panicking and scrambling toward the only exit, he realized that, with or without help, he now had personally to kill Washington. He removed the dagger from its sheath inside his jacket and calmly walked toward the unsuspecting Washington. The General, with his back to Chief Ohenton, was speaking rapidly to Chief Tackapousha.

Nathaniel, whose attention had been fixated on Chief Ohenton since the latter first entered the room, saw what was happening. As he pushed Washington out of the way, Nathaniel plunged his own dagger into the chest of the lunging Chief. With a look of astonished disbelief, the would-be assassin of General Washington, staggered and then fell to the floor. Outside, most of the attackers, had either been killed or captured except for a few Redcoats and Braves who were able to escape into the south woods.

Reacting in a way that surprised and upset Washington, the Continental Congress later decried the General's "foolhardy recklessness" in attending an "inconsequential" meeting which could have put his life and the colonial cause in jeopardy.

One well-known delegate in the Virginia legislature denounced the use of Indians to attack other Indians, as an occurrence unnecessarily foolhardy and one that "could offend" the probable allies of the British, the Iroquois, into possibly deciding to align themselves with the Algonquins and Patriots instead of the British. Many members of the Continental Congress agreed with him and voted to officially disregard, or at least, to minimize the incident. That is why there is little mention in the official governmental records of the meeting and the brave act of Nathaniel Townsend who had saved the life of General Washington and perhaps preserved the fight for American liberty. There is not even a mention of the battle in David Ramsay's biography, Life of George Washington, published almost a decade after Washington's death, on December 14, 1799, at Mount Vernon, Virginia.

The incident became, thus, less than a minor footnote in American history. But, on that morning of August 24, 1774, there was not censure but jubilation in foiling the plot to assassinate Washington and in defeating the British and the Narreckhewicks.

George Washington, however, was at the time well aware of the courage of Nathaniel in risking his life in order to save his. After conferring with his commanders and Chief Tackapousha, he approached Nathaniel and thanked him for his courageous action.

"There are not enough words at my command to thank you, Nathaniel. I have stared at the face of death many times, and for a few seconds this morning, I thought it would win. I am forever in your debt, my good friend." Washington put his hand on Nathaniel's shoulder, and in physical gestures he rarely made, he shook his hand and then embraced him.

"I want you to know, also, that Chief Tackapousha, who calls himself your Indian father, a situation which I do not yet fully understand, is very proud of you. In talking to him just now, he kept calling you 'my son, my son, the Golden Warrior.' Someday, Nathaniel, you will have to tell me the complete story why he calls you the 'Golden Warrior.'"

And one day, Nathaniel did.

CHAPTER 40
TRAIL'S END

After many historic military campaigns, the Colonial Army in a decisive battle defeated the British and General Charles Cornwallis at Yorktown, Virginia, on October 19, 1781. The resulting peace treaty, signed by Great Britain and the United States, ended the Revolutionary War. George Washington in 1789 was elected the first President of the United States, receiving 69 electoral votes to John Adams', 34.

Nathaniel served in various important governmental positions under the nation's first three Presidents: George Washington, John Adams, and Thomas Jefferson. Washington selected him to help establish and organize the first Bureau of Indian Affairs. When Adams appointed him as Assistant Ambassador to England, he and Jessie went to London.

In 1801, one of President Jefferson's first acts was to name Nathaniel to a position which is now called Assistant Secretary of State. Jefferson had noted that Nathaniel had been helpful not only in assessing the American Indian situation but also in negotiations leading to the Louisiana Purchase from France. Nathaniel and Jessie attended the ceremonies in New Orleans in 1803 to witness the transfer of the territory to the United States.

In 1804, at the age of 56, despite Jefferson's attempts to

dissuade him, Nathaniel resigned from government service. In their thirty years of marriage, he and Jessie had three children: Samuel, William, and, at the persistent urging of Jessie, their daughter was named Arandel. Samuel became famous for his stories about colonial life and the American Revolution. William made a career in business, and Arandel grew up to be a beautiful, blue-eyed blonde who eventually was told the sad story of her father and the Indian Princess whom she was named after.

The marriage of Daniel "Whaleman" and Martha, resulted, to their delight, in the conception of two children, Hannah and Daniel. Their son Daniel became the owner of two whaling companies, one at Sag Harbor and the other in Nantucket. When the industry began to vanish in the late 1840's, he studied to become a barrister. Hannah married an Army officer and travelled with him to various military posts throughout the young country. Despite the sadness and tragedy in her maternal grandmother's early life, which ended with her murder by an Indian, she became an advocate of Indian rights.

Shanghai Jim Chang, thanks to the influence of Nathaniel with President Washington, was given free passage on one of the whaling vessels circling South America's Cape Horn and sailing as far north as San Francisco. Shanghai Jim was permitted also at no charge, in San Francisco to board a federal ship, which was transporting American statesmen bound for China to explore trade possibilities between the two countries. Fortunately for Chang, the seven-masted schooner's next stop, after the seven - month voyage from New York, was Shanghai.

As the schooner moved slowly through the South China and East China Seas, Shanghai Jim's excitement steadily increased. It was difficult to believe that after so many years, he was finally returning to his beloved city of Shanghai, the "Paris of the East," even though he had been shanghaied there.

In the notorious city of sin and every other imaginable vice, he bought a building which he converted into a combination bar and restaurant. Shanghai Jim had saved some of the colonial tavern's net profits even after contributing to his share of the business expenses and to what he called "female entertainment" or as Whaleman once said to him: "Why don't you just call it what it is - sex!"

He named his Hunanese - type restaurant "Shanghai Jim's." At first, he did some of the bartending and cooking himself. After the restaurant became very successful, he hired professional bartenders, cooks, and scantily clad "bar girls" who, in addition to food and drinks, served sex in the back room for a reasonable price. The small rooms with beds were guarded by two burly Chinese men who admitted only the "bar girls" and their paying customers.

Many times Chang would look longingly at a corner table and imagine that perhaps someday Nathaniel, Whaleman, and he would be sitting and laughing there, recalling old memories and telling stories as they used to in their own colonial tavern in the New World.

He could almost hear Whaleman saying, "Why don't you get married, Shanghai? You got a lot of time on your hands. Pick out one of the squaws, at least!" And Shanghai would give him his usual answer: "Who would marry a Chinaman? Someday I'll go back to China and who here would come with me!"

A year later, Chang married a pretty Hong Kong woman who bore him seven children. It was incomprehensible to his wife, in-laws, and friends why he would give two un - Chinese names to two of his sons: Nathaniel and David. Every time he would call his two boys, he would start laughing - a habit which, at first puzzled his wife.

After travelling from New York City and then to Washington D.C., Nathaniel was appointed by Washington in 1789 to help establish the first Bureau of Indian Affairs. He visited, for the first time since his promotion, the grave site of his parents in a field outside Canarsies Town. He had always tried to remember as much as he could about his parents in the time before he was eight years old...

At Arandel's grave nearby, he thought he could still hear her teasing him, laughing at his mixed white man - Indian ways, and attempts to speak fluent Algonquin. In the early morning mist, he placed a red feather and a yellow one on her grave, and he imagined - or did he? – that he saw her face and that she was smiling at him and calling him "my Golden Warrior" - and Nathaniel smiled back and cried.

EPILOGUE

Washington's sincerity in promoting a policy of fair treatment of the American Indians included not only the Long Island and other New York territory Indians but also all the other Indian tribes west of the Appalachian Mountains. As early as 1789, the first year of his presidency, Washington tried to initiate and implement a treaty with the powerful and influential Western Creek Indians, but he was unsuccessful.

The next year Washington did not approve of the various strategies presented to him about annexing Western Indian land. Some politicians favored the use of unrestricted military force and others suggested a more gradual approach to confiscating Indian territory as pioneers moved westward. Some of Washington's closest advisers, including Nathaniel Townsend, suggested not only a series of fair and honorable peace treaties but also compensation for the Native Americans.

But, the overwhelming influx of American settlers reaching and then crossing the Mississippi River swept away any good intentions, including any previously established governmental treaties or agreements. The Native American Indians, reputedly inhabiting the land for 9,000 years, were rendered helpless against the unstoppable pioneer migration and the inability, despite their efforts, of the new American government to establish a fair Indian policy which would have enabled the Indian culture to survive and flourish.

Even Nathaniel Townsend, who played a relatively unknown but significant role in the new government, was unable, as were the three Presidents he served under, to develop an equitable Indian policy. That is why in frustration after fifteen years of government service, Nathaniel retired in 1804.

His biographer noted that the evening before his retirement, Nathaniel had walked through the streets of Washington, the new capital, and reminisced with Jessie about the happy "early days" with his parents, friends, Chief Tackapousha, and the beautiful Indian Princess, Arandel.

But he still could not forget…

POSTSCRIPT

In 1780, on September 16, George Washington wrote a letter to his Chief of Intelligence, Major Benjamin Tallmadge, asking that Oyster Bay's Robert Townsend (no relation to Nathaniel Townsend), also one of his principal spies, be recognized for his duty as an American spy.

Washington also wrote a letter to Nathaniel Townsend, commending him for saving his life and for his efforts in spying for the colonists. A copy of this letter was filed in the secret governmental archives where it still remains today.

Because of my neighbor and friend who, many decades ago, told me about Arandel, I am able to tell you the true story of the unsung heroism of Nathaniel Townsend and his love for the Indian Princess, Arandel, who helped develop him into a man and who inspired him to reach the potential of his courage.

S.S.

Digital ID: pga 01593 Reproduction Number: LC-DIG-pga-01593 Library of
Congress Prints and Photographs Division Washington, D.C. 20540 USA

Author's Previous Novel

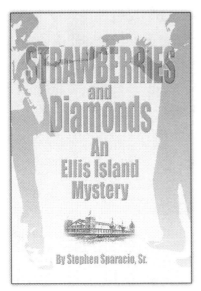

Dr. Sparacio's previous novel, *Strawberries and Diamonds, An Ellis Island Mystery,* published in 2008, is available at the author's website, *www.trafford.com/07-3053,* or at most major online book sellers. It can also be ordered at a local bookstore or directly from the publisher: *orders@trafford.com.*

The novel is about two poor and desperate Sicilians who rob a famous upscale jewelry store in Rome in 1913. They attempt to smuggle the gemstones, mostly diamonds, by emigrating to America via an immigrant ship and Ellis Island. On the journey, tragedy befalls the two, but not before the jewels, to avoid confiscation in Customs, are hidden in the main building on Ellis Island.

Almost a hundred years later, a private detective and a Chinese assassin search for the jewels and, in a life-or-death confrontation in the cold falling snow on the deserted and neglected southern end of Ellis Island, a fatal mistake determined the survivor.

In a ForeWord Clarion Book Review, the critic wrote that the novel tells a "successful story…is well researched and painstakingly plotted." The novel, *"Strawberries and Diamonds, An Ellis Island Mystery,* has beautifully written flashbacks and provides rich details and descriptions of the conditions that poverty-stricken immigrants were subjected to on the two-week voyage across the Atlantic…such descriptions put the reader into the story…the author has created some memorable characters…" (May, 2009)